THE SPIDER:
LABORATORY OF THE DAMNED

THE SPIDER

MASTER OF MEN!

LABORATORY OF THE DAMNED

By Grant Stockbridge

STEEGER BOOKS • 2020

CHAPTER 1
LIVING DEAD MAN

THE SIRENS were still purring when the four police-men swung hastily from their motorcycles. Their shoving bodies and raucous shouts broke a lane through the curious crowd and they leaned their shoulders against the press of humans and, holding people back, waited. An imported sedan swished to a halt at the curb and before the bearded Hindu footman could open his door, a man surged out of the tonneau.

There was a purposeful forward thrust to his shoulders. His lean face was drawn by harsh lines; his gray-blue eyes held a searching intentness. They stabbed once to the right, once to the left and every man and woman in the crowd felt the impact personally. Then he was bounding up the steps of the hospital. The heavy doors shivered at the hurried vehemence of his entry.

A grave-faced young man fell into step with him. His manner was diffident. "I'm Dr. Moreland, Mr. Wentworth," he explained quietly. "Commissioner Kirkpatrick had a brief period of consciousness about ten minutes ago. He is in a coma again now, but we may expect...."

Richard Wentworth cut him short with an impatient wave of his hand as they stepped into the elevator. "Yes, yes! I received all those particulars by radio. But has he spoken? Who is suspected?"

Dr. Moreland repeated blankly, "Who is suspected? I don't understand...."

Wentworth's lips twitched. "The commissioner of the New York City police, a man noted for his implacable warfare on criminals, is stricken abruptly by a disease which falls into no

Their faces were blue, and they lolled in the clutch of death!

known category. The only word he has been able to utter during his brief periods of consciousness has been my name. I also am known for my bitter hostility to crime...."

"You are also his friend, sir," Dr. Moreland interrupted, hesitantly. "It is natural...."

The elevator door opened and Dr. Moreland led the way swiftly along the muted hallway of the hospital. Wentworth's lips had grown into a harsher line. Friends...? Yes, he and Kirkpatrick were that—as fiercely loyal to each other as brothers should be. But Kirkpatrick had summoned him for no such reason as that. He was not a man to ask friends to—console him in illness. There was a deeper motive, a more sinister explanation than that. Why else had a deadly attempt been made on Wentworth's own life the very day after Kirkpatrick had been stricken?

Wentworth's eyes briefly surveyed the set, almost stubborn profile of the young doctor striding beside him. In attendance upon Kirkpatrick, the man fell under suspicion. More than that, he was a man to watch with wary eyes. Wentworth had no doubt that the men who had struck at Kirkpatrick were the same who had made that attempt on him; it was unlikely they would quit after only one try....

The doctor—Moreland he had called himself, Wentworth remembered—opened a door and stood aside. There was evident resentment in his bearing, a more stubborn out-thrust of his jaw....

The room he entered was the antechamber of a hospital suite, fitted as a luxurious sitting-room. Two women stood at a window across the room, one trim in a nurse's starched white, the other dressed in a severely tailored suit of silk which failed to mask the sweeping, fine lines of her body.

The nurse said, "You're to go right in, Mr. Wentworth. Doctor Hess and Doctor Higgins are already there."

The other woman met his stabbing gaze with veiled eyes. There was no color in her face except the scarlet line of her mouth, which was full, but, somehow, not soft. There was a square line to her jaw that indicated will power; intelligence showed in the thin-bridged nose. She smiled slowly. At Wentworth's elbow, Moreland muttered. "You've heard of Doctor Magda Hess…?"

WENTWORTH NODDED, his eyes lighting. "Like to talk to you after I see Kirkpatrick," he said swiftly. "Your reputation in experimental toxicology is quite equal to that of your father."

The girl—she was really little more than that—flushed under his praise, a dusky rose touching her cheekbones. "You are more than kind," she replied, her voice low. "I'll be glad to wait, though father is really supervising the case."

Wentworth's eyes sharpened as he strode toward the door to the inner room. Dr. Johnson Hess was the city toxicologist, reputed to be one of the most able scientists in the field of poisons that had ever lived. If he were "supervising" the case, there must be suspicions of which young Moreland knew nothing. It meant, almost beyond a doubt, that the attempt on Wentworth's life had been made with poisons also….

Kirkpatrick lay with a pale motionlessness which was deathlike. Only the faint, slow movement of breathing proved that he still lived. The two doctors stood together on one side of the bed, Hess with his stooped shoulders, his long, white hair and his fragile face which was more that of a musician than of an expert in poisons; Higgins erect, militant, his red hair bristling as if in individual defiance....

"Wentworth," he nodded in greeting. "Can expect consciousness in twenty-three minutes. Duration two minutes; coma again."

Wentworth stood motionless, staring down at the face of his friend. The features held the sharpness of death, the muscles and flesh sagging beneath the skin, drawing it taut over the nasal bridge, away from the cheekbones. Wentworth's mouth twitched once, but otherwise his own face was utterly without expression. Except that, when he lifted his head, his eyes were twin pits of flame.

"Higgins," his voice croaked out, "you suspect poison. Why?"

Higgins met his eyes with a direct belligerence. "It's not disease, not a functional, glandular or mental disorder. Nothing left but poison." Higgins and Wentworth always fought like that, but there was a deep affinity between the two men. Wentworth had served him mightily once and Higgins was not a man to forget easily.

"What poison, Hess?" Wentworth demanded.

The older man jerked about, his hands shaking at the abrupt challenge. His voice was mild, without emphasis. "I know of none to produce this change, Mr. Wentworth," he said. "There are some that produce complete catalepsis, some which have a cataleptic stage immediately preceding death. But I know of none which would maintain a static catalepsis." His old eyes were a brilliant blue, but somehow they wavered and could not quite meet those of the stern young man across the bed.

Higgins held out a long, brown envelope which he drew from his inner pocket. Wentworth took it silently, found that it had been addressed in Kirkpatrick's vigorous, vertical script: *To be delivered to Richard Wentworth in the event of my death or disability.*

That last word snagged Wentworth's thoughts. So Kirkpatrick had anticipated not only death but some such thing as had already happened to him. Wentworth's fingers were very steady as he ripped open the tough manila, but compression made his lips pale. Within was a single, closely written sheet of paper. It was headed: Cases of Poisoning!

UNDER IT were listed seven names, all of them, Wentworth saw, those of wealthy persons who either had died or had been stricken with paralysis during the last month. At the end was a notation indicating that toxicologist examinations had revealed no trace of drugs—followed by a single phrase, heavily under-scored: *Remove Hess!*

Wentworth looked up from the paper to his friend's expres-sionless face, which showed the harsh determination of the man even when it bore the blank emptiness of death. What fearful thing had Kirkpatrick stumbled on in this list of names? The answer came with stunning force. He had discovered the truth! Why else should he have been stricken down with this ailment—so like the paralysis which apparently had felled three of the seven persons on his list? A murder plot of huge proportions…? Wentworth whipped about, his eyes burning into the mild, tremulous-lipped face of Dr. Hess, the city toxicologist whom Kirkpatrick had intended to have removed because—the answer was in Hess's failure to find poison—because Kirkpatrick suspected him of complicity!

Higgins spoke sharply, "He's stirring!"

Wentworth bent over the inert body of his friend. Stirring, they called it, but there was no motion in that gaunt, powerful frame. There was a feeble twitching of eyelids, a jerking of the muscles of the face. It warped Kirkpatrick's countenance terribly. The mouth twisted sideways, the lips quivered and there was a spasmodic working of his throat.

"He can't hear, I understand," Wentworth said swiftly to Higgins, "nor speak. But you believe him rational when he is conscious?"

"Yes," Higgins' voice rasped. "He might even be able to read."

Wentworth was already scribbling on the back of the message from Kirkpatrick—large, clearly formed letters: *Is Hess with poisoners? Blink your eyes once for yes, twice for no.*"

He finished, stood waiting. His right hand knotted into a hard fist. This was torment, watching Kirkpatrick struggle for consciousness. It was plain that only his indomitable will dragged him up from the depths of the coma in which he lay most of the time. His face muscles writhed, his mouth opened in a silent scream and, heavily, as if their weight were incredible, the eyelids were forced upward. For a space of seconds, the eyes thus revealed were glazed, without sight. Then they focused sharply on Wentworth's face. A glad light leaped into them, a fury of joy which was shocking in its intensity.

Wentworth forced himself to smile and nodded. He moved his lips in soundless words: "I'll take care of you, Kirk. I'll get the poisoners." He held the message he had written before Kirkpatrick's eyes.

Two minutes of consciousness, Higgins had said. For two short minutes out of each hour, Kirkpatrick fought his way back. The seconds were speeding. His eyes strained at the message as if it were a struggle to force their meaning into his brain. His eyes flew back to Wentworth's face and his mouth writhed, his whole face convulsed with the effort to speak. Sweat beaded Wentworth's forehead as he watched; his fists knotted at his sides, but he forced his lips to move normally.

"Wink, Kirkpatrick. Once for yes; twice for no."

The eyes glared unwinking into Wentworth's face, and the incredible writhing of Kirkpatrick's facial muscles increased. Wentworth cursed.

"For God's sake, Kirk," he whispered. "Stop trying, stop trying…!"

A HOARSE sound was forced from Kirkpatrick's throat. It was incredible, inhuman, as if a dog had tried to pronounce a word. There was a guttural ghost of a "d" sound, a vowel that was indistinguishable and another consonant that might be "d" or "t," or Kirkpatrick made the sound again. His face reddened as if he were screaming at the top of his voice. His chest heaved as he panted; his eyes protruded; he collapsed. The muscles went limp and his eyes rolled up in their sockets, the lids fluttered shut. Wentworth gasped out a breath he had been holding….

"Thank God! Oh, thank God!" he whispered.

Higgins said, with a dry rasp. "I don't think I'd ask him that question again, Wentworth, unless you want to kill him."

Wentworth jerked his head in negation. He snatched up the nurse's report sheet, ripped a piece of paper from it and wrote again. He gave it to Higgins.

"The next time he regains consciousness, show him that," he ordered curtly.

Deliberately, Higgins read the message. He nodded. "That's wise, to tell him that you got his word. But did you?"

Wentworth nodded grimly, his eyes burning into the averted face of the white-haired Dr. Hess. "I got his message," he said shortly. "Hess, I want to speak to you in the other room."

Wentworth ushered the older man from the bedside with a hard-faced courtesy. If this bluff failed, he had nothing to work on at all—no source of investigation. What Kirkpatrick had tried to convey he had no idea at all, but one thing was clear. He had denied that he suspected Hess. Yet neither had he indicated that the man was guilty, and he had had the use of his eyelids. If he could muster his strength sufficiently to make a sound in his throat, he was able to move his eyelids.

"Your patient needs you," he told the nurse shortly.

At the tone of his voice, Magda Hess faced abruptly toward him. She stepped alertly to her father's side, her movements graceful, the line of her body long and lithe. Wentworth eyed the two, father and daughter, with a direct, stern gaze. He held out Kirkpatrick's message to the man.

"Read that," he commanded, "and then tell me what you make of the note at the end of the message. It says, *'Remove Hess!'* "

The doctor's veined hand trembled as he reached for the paper. It rattled and Wentworth felt impatience within him. This man could not be guilty of poisonings. Men his age had no desires which were strong enough to urge them to murder, unless... unless... Wentworth's eyes turned to the defiant face of the girl. Could it be that the doctor would be willing to throw his incredible knowledge of poisonings into criminal hands for her sake? To build a vast, illicit fortune for her? He knew without question that there were criminals who would pay huge sums for the deadly knowledge Dr. Hess possessed....

Dr. Hess held out the paper. "I do not understand," he muttered, his voice quavering. "I really do not understand. These men whose names he lists, those whose organs I examined, all died of poison. I am reasonably sure they died of poison, from the condition of the organs. But I could not discover the kind of poison, nor any traces of it. That's the report I made to the Commissioner."

"You reported that these men were poisoned?" Wentworth demanded sharply. "But you see Kirkpatrick's notes. In each case, he says 'natural death, toxicologist verdict.'"

Dr. Hess' white head shook. It made strands of his long hair dangle across his bulging forehead and his daughter brushed it aside with tender fingers.

"You should be ashamed," she said, her voice quivering with

emotion, "to torture an old man like this. What he says is true. He made a report of poisoning in each of those cases and I can show you carbon copies with his signature. We keep a copy of each one."

Wentworth frowned, two vertical creases making his brow stern, "You realize what you are saying?" be warned curtly. "That these reports were tampered with at police headquarters? That would be virtually impossible. Especially in a case in which the Commissioner was directly interested."

MAGDA HESS lifted one shoulder in a shrug which was at once insolent and attractive. "I will show you the carbon copies," she promised clearly. "Come, father. It is clear that if Mr. Wentworth suspects you, your advice will not be accepted in Kirkpatrick's case. You won't require a consultation, I take it?"

She led her father to the door. Moreland came out of Kirkpatrick's room, into which he had gone with the nurse.

"Just a moment, doctor!" he called. His manner was utterly diffident. It was plain that he respected the aged scientist greatly. "Doctor Hess, I have suggested to Dr. Higgins that we might use the antidote sometimes employed against *curare*, the poison which has a similar effect, except that the paralysis precedes death only briefly, and...."

Magda interrupted Moreland's eager flow of words sharply. "Dr. Hess has withdrawn from the Kirkpatrick case," she announced bitterly. "Hereafter, Mr. Wentworth is in charge."

Wentworth stood silent, his gaze never leaving the group at the door, but his mind was racing with conjecture. The girl's reaction was natural enough under the circumstances. Her father's integrity had been questioned....

"I will send for those copies of the reports," he said. "Photostats will do."

Magda Hess nodded, her lips scornful. She led her father from the room and Wentworth felt the glare from the younger doctor. Moreland was scowling. His hair was dark red, waving back from his forehead, worn rather long.

"You're taking a big responsibility on yourself, Mr. Wentworth," he greeted. "There isn't another man in the world who can equal Dr. Hess' knowledge."

"True," Wentworth acknowledged, "but can one be sure that he will employ it only for the patient's benefit?"

Moreland seemed, for a moment, stunned by the implication. Wentworth, studying his face narrowly, was certain that the young doctor was not acting. His amazement was succeeded by anger. He took a long stride forward.

"I should thrash hell out of you for that," Moreland said coldly, "but I probably couldn't do it."

"That's right." Wentworth smiled slightly.

Moreland flushed. "Nevertheless, if you repeat the insult against Dr. Hess, I'll make an attempt."

Wentworth bowed slightly, still smiling. In spite of himself—in spite of the man's association with Hess—he could not help a surge of liking for Moreland. The fellow had taken his goading in a level-headed, intelligent manner. His courtesy and his courage were equal.

WENTWORTH CAREFULLY folded the paper Kirk-

13

patrick had left him and slid it into the inside pocket of his dark tweed lounge-suit. "At another time," he said pleasantly, "I'd like to discuss the matter further with you. For the present, I find myself occupied." He nodded, started past Moreland.

The doctor sprang in front of Wentworth. "Just a minute," he said hoarsely. "I don't want you to think I'm afraid of you."

Wentworth smiled quizzically into his face. "I really made no such imputation," he said. "I don't doubt your courage—only your wisdom."

Moreland struck swiftly, but Wentworth merely moved his head slightly and the blow slid over his shoulder. He tapped Moreland lightly in the solar plexus with his left fist, on the point of the jaw with his right. They were not blows, merely taps, to show what could have been done. Moreland stepped back, bowing, his face pale.

"I beg your pardon," he said stiffly, "I forgot myself."

"Quite," Wentworth agreed. He bowed and went on into the hall, but his smile faded as he went and once more a vertical crease dented his forehead. He was sure that Moreland was too spontaneous, too young to be capable of alliance with the ruthless criminals who must be behind the poisonings Kirkpatrick had discovered. Doctor Hess' position was curious, if he had actually made the reports as he said. Wentworth was abruptly certain that he would find this to be the case, and....

He stepped out on the sidewalk in front of the hospital. There were still a few curious people standing around. Two of the policemen were lounging against the fender of Wentworth's car, two others astride their motorcycles, balancing them with their feet. As he came out of the door, one of them kicked his motor to life.

The turbaned Hindu who had driven the car moved swiftly to the door of the car and threw it open. Wentworth strode across the walk, abruptly making up his mind. He would reach Hess' home and laboratory before the man and his daughter arrived, search the records… He saw that the man who had come to meet him at the docks, the one who had discovered Kirkpatrick's sudden illness, was still lounging in the rear of the Daimler, smoking. He'd have to get rid of the man; Jan Vanderveer was his name. He had made a living, Wentworth recalled, by acting as private detective for various society friends since the depression had wiped out his own considerable fortune….

Wentworth put his foot on the step of the car, nodded to the Hindu, ordered him in swift Punjabi to go to the Hess home. He smiled at Vanderveer, glanced out the window on the opposite side, and a cry rose, stranglingly, in his throat. He could see the motorcycle policeman's face very clearly. It was drained of all color, eyes blazing wide with fear. His heavy police revolver was leveled at Wentworth's chest at a range of not more than two yards! Even as Wentworth glimpsed his twisted face, the man began shooting…!

CHAPTER 2
THE DOCTOR'S CELLAR

A MAN cannot move his body as rapidly as his arms, nor drop as swiftly as he can move to the side. These were things that Wentworth knew from long necessity from years of his life lived in the constant shadow of peril where reflex action, rather than thought, must save him. But reflexes can be trained, and Wentworth spent idle hours of every day at that work. It was his reflexes which operated when he saw the leveled gun and the white, fearful face of the policeman which he knew heralded an attempt at assassination.

Wentworth's right hand was grasping the central door-post of the car, steadying him as he bent his head to enter the tonneau. It was the leverage of that arm which he used. He contracted it, using the speed of his arm, rather than the muscles of his body, to hurl himself sideways out of the range of the gun, into the shelter of the car itself. The first jerk of his arm moved him aside from the first bullet, then the powerful muscles of his body came into play and pulled him down.

The gun continued to hammer. Wentworth had been forced to fall on his right arm, but his left was free and it darted to the automatic which nestled under his right armpit. It was madness to attempt to shoot at the man while gun-fire filled the door-way with lead. Wentworth peered under the car. The man's feet were not visible, but the tires of his motorcycle were. Wentworth exploded the rear tire with a single shot, then the motor roared and the cycles spurted forward. Wentworth sprang erect, gun ready, saw that the policeman, despite the flat tire, had wheeled about and was racing diagonally across the avenue toward a side street.

Wentworth recognized instantly that if he took time to dart toward the rear of the sedan, the motorcycle would gain the cover of the side street—He clapped a hand to the mudguard, vaulted to the hood and was instantly on balance, his forty-five automatic lining steadily on the fleeing policeman's back. The man twisted a white face about and knew Wentworth had him pinned. He swerved, did sliding fandangos with his machine, but it

was not that which caused Wentworth to lower his weapon.

It was quite clear that this was no madman's trick, but a planned attempt on his life. Obviously it was the work of the same men who had struck Kirkpatrick down. Here was a thing more important even than searching Hess' records. Wentworth sprang to the earth on the left side of the car, whipped open the door and sprang to the wheel. It was at this moment that he realized that at least one of the bullets had struck his Hindu body servant, Ram Singh. The Sikh was gripping his right arm, his teeth shining fiercely and bravely through his bushy beard….

"Get into the hospital!" Wentworth shouted at him. His foot kicked the starter and the powerful motor caught instantly. He whirled the Daimler in a tight u-turn, bumped up over the opposite curbing, and within five seconds after the policeman's last shot, he was in pursuit of the fleeing man. Behind him, he heard motorcycles pop into life, knew that they would join the pursuit. His lips moved in silent curses. They must not be allowed to shoot the assassin. He threw a glance over his shoulder and, for the first time, remembered that Vanderveer was still

17

in the rear seat. The lanky society detective was crawling forward through the window which separated him from the front seat.

"I say!" he cried. "That was jolly good ducking, what, what?"

He slipped into the seat beside Wentworth, tucked his monocle back into his eye and slipped an automatic from an underarm holster. He flipped open the lock to see there was a cartridge in the chamber, laid it on his knee and smiled, rather fatuously.

"I say, shall I pot the beggar?" he cried above the engine-roar, brandishing the automatic. "I'm rather handy with these deuced things."

Wentworth shook his head. "Want to follow him!" he shouted. "Somebody put him up to that."

"Oh, quite, quite!" Vanderveer agreed.

WENTWORTH SAT back negligently behind the wheel of the speeding car. The car ahead was using his siren to clear a path and it was merely a matter of following the "beggar." Wentworth began to know exhilaration. Dealing with poisoners was a grim, oppressive business, but the direct attack of bullets he could understand and relish. The blood pumped with a pleasant warmth through his veins.

"If any of those motorcycle cops pulls alongside!" he called. "Tell them to leave the man ahead alone. They can use their sirens, but not their guns!"

"Oh, righto!" Vanderveer agreed. He opened the door of the car and stood on the running board, an arm linked through the door-post. He held the gun in his hand, the monocle still was screwed firmly into his eye.

Wentworth laughed. He had been inclined to be a little

condescending about Vanderveer's private detective business, but it was quite plain that the man had courage, despite his foppish appearance. A motorcycle roared up alongside and Vanderveer shouted Wentworth's message and got it over. The cop spurted to a position ten feet ahead of the Daimler and stayed there, his siren shrilling.

How the fugitive managed to stay on his motorcycle with its flat tire, Wentworth could not understand. But he did manage it, although racing on the rim precluded any fast turns and the man apparently knew it. He traveled in a straight line, and had made only two slow turns, both of them to the right, so that they were now speeding back toward the East River.

They were two blocks from South Street, which bordered the river, when the thing happened. There was no warning at all except the keen eyesight of an experienced driver like Wentworth. He glimpsed movement on his left side, in the entrance of a garage and what occurred after that was too swift for thought. He realized that the truck loaded with steel beams, which projected far over its rear, would completely fill the street before he could get past. It would not be possible to stop in time to prevent a collision. Vanderveer let out a shrill warning yelp and jumped to the street even as Wentworth slapped on brakes.

Wentworth's hand closed on the door handle beside him. He threw himself sideways, clinging to the door, and the steel beams came crashing through the windshield, through the entire car to burst out through its back. Any human in the path of these girders would have been mashed to a jelly....

The impact, the abrupt cessation of forward movement,

19

whipped Wentworth about like the lash of a whip. When the door slammed open to its fullest extent, Wentworth was snapped loose and sent rolling, straight toward the wheels of the truck. He contrived to convert the force of his throw into a rotary motion so that his body was spinning on its longitudinal axis when he struck the ground. He was half stunned by the force of the landing. Pain knifed through his back, but he had saved

... steel beams came crashing

through the windshield....

his head from striking. He saw dazedly, helplessly, that he was plunging straight toward the wheels of the truck, which still moved backward with the momentum and gigantic weight of its load. It was impossible to stop. Wentworth did not try. He increased the vigor of his rolling, aiding impulse of his fall with every muscle of his body. He shot under the truck, brought up against the opposite curb of the street and staggered to his feet. HE REELED forward, lips skinned back from clenched teeth. His head was whirling. Within a few moments, he would be violently ill from shock. He might become unconscious, but while his senses remained to him… He reached the cab of the truck, grasped the handrail, and pulled himself upward. The driver jerked about toward him, eyes flaring wide at sight of the gun in Wentworth's hand. Wentworth did not shoot. He struck, snatched the unconscious man to his shoulder and staggered up the street.

A taxi driver had left his cab and was running back toward him. "Quick," Wentworth gasped. "Get this injured man into your cab!"

The taxi driver took the unconscious truck man and Wentworth sagged into the back seat. The driver sprang to the seat.

"Bellevue hospital's nearest!" he shouted.

"No hospital," Wentworth returned harshly. "I want that motorcycle cop who went past just before the crack-up!"

The driver twisted about, saw Wentworth's grim face, the gun in his hand. He yelped, stepped on the accelerator and got away fast. "I'll find him!" he squealed. "Don't shoot, Chief, I'll find him!"

Wentworth sagged back against the cushions panting and shaken. The world swam darkly before his eyes. Nausea pounded at his stomach... It was minutes before he began to feel half-way normal again. Any man less accustomed to violence and to rapid action would have passed out cold. He threw back his head, sucked in deep, long breaths. The taxi driver stared back, face still white and frightened.

"I can't find that lousy cop!" he yelled. "I swear I been trying!"

Wentworth peered out the window and saw that they had been doubling back and were almost on the street where the accident had occurred.

"All right," he said. "Back to the scene."

He paid the driver well, stared speculatively at the unconscious truck driver. "Think you could keep an eye on that guy for me?" he asked.

"Sure!" the driver said eagerly. "Sure I can."

Wentworth nodded, "It's worth another twenty if you do," he said, and walked, still a little unsteadily, back toward where the truck still jammed the street. There was an ambulance down there, a crowd that eddied and swirled. He pushed through it resolutely, and realized for the first time that the motorcycle policeman who had been ahead of him hadn't missed the truck. One of the beam ends had caught him in the chest and another had taken his head off. And Vanderveer... He turned his face

23

away from the corpse that was being covered with a sheet by the ambulance man, walked toward the interne.

"Another casualty in here?" he asked, nodding toward the ambulance.

The interne was smoking a pipe and he couldn't make the thing draw right. His hands were shaking. "One casualty," he said. He cursed raggedly. "And that's enough, by God! I've seen some pretty messy accidents…."

"Hey, mister!" a boy's voice volunteered "A man went into that doctor's office over there. Funny guy with a monocle…."

WENTWORTH WENT where the boy pointed. Vanderveer couldn't be very badly hurt if he'd managed to cling to his monocle. His estimation of Vanderveer rose a notch. A man had to know how to leap from a speeding car without injuring himself… He stopped at the steps which led up to the doctor's office, a neat little two-story brick building, with the entrance to the office beside the main door. He looked at the brass-and-black sign and he caught his breath. His eyes narrowed. The name read:

Thomas Moreland, M. D.

It couldn't be coincidence. This was undoubtedly the same Thomas Moreland who had been in Kirkpatrick's room. It was queer, too, that the accident had happened in front of his office. Wentworth's lips took on a grim line as he pressed the bell beside the name-plate and opened the office door. A girl in a nurse's uniform was coming toward him.

"Oh!" she cried. "You were in the accident, too? Come into

the office. The doctor isn't in, but I can do a first-aid job…" She smiled and Wentworth saw that there was a deep dimple at each corner of her mouth and that her eyes were blue and gay. "Iodine and adhesive," she said, confidentially. "You're not badly hurt, are you?"

Vanderveer, struggling into his coat, showed in the door of the inner office. "Oh, I say," he cried. "This is ripping! I was afraid you were jolly well mashed up…" The monocle was still in his eyes. The knee of one trouser leg was ripped across and under it, there was an adhesive patch. There was a long panel mirror on one wall and Wentworth looked at himself in it and abruptly grinned. Yes, it was quite plain he had been in an accident. He turned to the girl. "I think iodine and adhesive will do very nicely," he said cheerfully.

Behind his smile, his mind reviewed the situation swiftly. Dr. Thomas Moreland was a friend and devotee of Hess; seemed very much interested also in the toxicologist's daughter. And now a truck loaded with beams, obviously by prearrangement, had backed into the path of the pursuing automobile at a point directly opposite Moreland's office… Wentworth looked keenly at the nurse. Her hands were agile and efficient as she dabbed iodine on a knee abrasion, made a sterile pad for it beneath the adhesive. She was serious, a small frown of concentration between her blue eyes. Her rich brown hair was rebellious in the confines of her nurse's cap. She patted the bandage.

"There. Are there any more cuts?" She looked up with a smile. Wentworth smiled back. "Virginia?" he said.

The girl flushed, then laughed. "And I thought I'd lost my

25

Southern accent! Yes, you're right. Richmond. I..." Her voice went dead, her eyes flaring wide as she stared over Wentworth's shoulder. He whipped about, hand flying to the automatic beneath his arm, and a low oath of surprise forced its way between his lips.

White-faced, staring at him from the half-opened door that led from the office into the doctor's house was—*the policeman assassin who had tried to kill Wentworth!*

CHAPTER 3
A MAN DIES TWICE

WENTWORTH HAD twisted to his left as he ripped out his automatic. He was ready to shoot, but the policeman had started backward at sight of the girl's staring eyes. He was out of sight a split-second after Wentworth's eyes brushed over him. The chair popped out from under Wentworth, crashed to the floor and skidded. He reached the doorway in two strides, glimpsed a heel and a hand gripping a corner of the wall as the policeman ducked from sight.

The gun at Wentworth's side spoke almost without volition and the hand popped out of sight. A man cried out in shrill pain and feet banged with a stumbling, irregular gait down steps, into a basement. There was a vertical crease between Wentworth's narrowed eyes as he bounded toward the head of the cellar stairway. Strange that a man would duck into a *cul de sac* from which there was no escape. But there might be an outside door... There was a chance of ambush, of course, but the man would have to

26

use a gun with his left hand. That right wouldn't be good for much after a half inch pellet of lead had smashed through it.

Wentworth ducked his head to clear the ceiling and leaped the whole length of the steps, plunged to his knees. A bullet fanned his cheek and tinkled through a window. The flash came from a far corner and there was the stealthy, retreating rasp of feet, barely audible amid the crashing echoes of the shot. Wentworth held his fire, sped soft-footed toward the sound. He whipped a small flashlight from his pocket, held it wide from his body as he flashed it on....

The beam pinned the policeman against a cement wall. His right hand dangled helpless at his side, his gun had been thrust through his belt and his left seemed to grope over the surface of the concrete.

"All right," Wentworth ordered quietly. "Keep that left hand up and turn around."

The man was rigid. He stood through a long half minute without even turning his face about, then he pivoted stiffly toward Wentworth. And he smiled. He knew he was looking Death in the eye, yet he smiled. His expression was almost triumphant, faintly derisive. He brushed his cap back off his forehead with his left hand, pressed the knuckles against his mouth as he yawned; then brought his teeth together with a queer snap. He held the left hand up and walked toward Wentworth.

"You've got me, Wentworth," he said casually, "but it ain't going to do you much good."

Wentworth's reply was measured, deliberate. "There is no one

RICHARD WENTWORTH

in the house who can or will interfere with anything I do. You understand me…? *with anything I do!*"

The man still grinned, but there was grayness beneath his swarthy skin. He swayed a little on his feet, his hand swung down, but with a limpness that was devoid of threat. "Sure," he whispered. "Sure, but you'd... better make... it quick!" He took a staggering step forward, then went down like a felled tree, stiffly, gathering speed. His face hit the floor with a sickening crunch, bounced. After that he did not move....

Wentworth stared down in amazement at the man. No one had injured him, yet he had all the appearance of having fallen dead! Behind him, Vanderveer's odd, British accents rang excitedly; his feet fumbled for the steps. He heard the sound of the girl's voice, but no words.

FROM THE fallen assassin, Wentworth glanced toward the cement wall. He had not suspected the man of trickery. No one could deliberately injure his face as that man had for an effect. There was no opening visible in the wall....

Vanderveer strode lankily to his side. "Oh, I say!" he cried delightedly. "You bagged the beggar!"

Wentworth shook his head slowly. "I only shot him through the hand. He was talking, and fell...." He stared at the policeman's left hand and abruptly he flung himself down on his knees, concentrating the direct, dazzling beam of the light on the twisted left hand of the officer. There was a ring that which had held a heavy stone. The stone was missing now, and Went-

29

worth was remembering that the cop's employer was a fiend who dealt in poisons. The man had snapped his teeth together while apparently patting a yawn with his knuckles.... Wentworth got slowly to his feet.

"Rings that contain poison have been used since Cleopatra's time," he growled heavily, "and probably before that."

"By Jove!" Vanderveer exclaimed. "You mean that the chappie took poison when you cornered him here? Fancy that!"

Wentworth jerked his head impatiently. He knew that Vanderveer's mannerisms were not affectation. A real man lay beneath all that. Nevertheless, he found them vaguely irritating. Even for a man educated at Eton and Oxford, that exaggerated accent seemed slightly false. Vanderveer bent his long body, prodded the cop's corpse with a rigid forefinger. Wentworth was still aware of the nurse's voice. It was nearer, now, and a man's tones rumbled with it. He turned as feet sounded on the steps and met the challenging, slightly belligerent gaze of Dr. Thomas Moreland. The nurse, just behind him, held a large vial in her hand....

Moreland strode to the officer's side without a word of greeting, turned him over on his back and sought a pulse, worked an eyelid with a forefinger. He opened a black bag he carried, rapidly assembled a hypodermic. Then he hesitated... glanced up at Wentworth.

"I was about to use adrenalin," he said, "assuming heart failure."

He did as Vanderveer had done, prodded with a rigid finger,

tried to bend an arm and leg. They were oddly stiff for a newly dead man. Moreland looked up again.

"What happened?"

Wentworth was frowning intently, his gray-blue eyes keen. Moreland had plainly said that he intended to remain near Kirkpatrick to make—with the attendant nurse and physician—the detailed diagnosis of the case. Yet he was here at his home within a few minutes of Wentworth's own arrival, though the pursuit had been at top speed. His eyes never leaving Moreland's challenging gaze, Wentworth told him briefly about the poison ring. Moreland's lips grinned.

"The vial, Miss Tarbell," he said curtly. He inserted the needle into the vial she held, filled it while he talked. "I came to get this preparation for possible use on the Commissioner. Dr. Higgins and I had almost decided to make the experiment. In certain cases of epilepsy and catalepsis, natural, it has been used to great advantage. I identify in this policeman many of the earlier symptoms of Kirkpatrick's case—except that it is plain that this man's case is more severe. As I understand it, this man attempted to kill you, Mr. Wentworth?"

Wentworth said slowly, "You propose to try this medication's effect on a criminal?"

Moreland nodded. His needle was ready. He pulled aside the already loosened clothing over the policeman's heart. "To all intents and purposes, the man is already dead. What I propose to attempt might be called resurrection."

THERE WAS still that crooked, mirthless grin upon his lips. Wentworth stepped abruptly forward, watching closely as the needle was run its full depth directly into the heart. His lips were grim, but the frown had not left his forehead. There was something more than queer about this entire business. To his own mind, there was inadequate reason to suspect that the policeman had used the catalepsis drug upon himself. There was the fact that the man apparently had been fumbling over the concrete wall at the end of the basement. To Wentworth

that indicated, abruptly, that there might be an opening there. It would not be the first time criminals had constructed underground hideouts with hidden doors....

The plunger of the hypodermic had been pressed home; the needle withdrawn. Moreland squatted, watching the man keenly. Without any preliminary warning, the policeman's eyes flew wide and he jerked erect. His left hand clutched at his heart.

"God," he whispered. "God... You double-cro—" His words ended in a rattling groan and he flopped heavily back to the earth, writhed convulsively.

Moreland worked swiftly, made a second injection, but it was of no avail. He rose slowly to his feet, threw his crooked grin at Wentworth.

"Just as well I tried it on the dog, don't you think?" he asked gently.

Wentworth stared at the man with a hard concentration that he made no attempt to disguise. By his own words, the man had declared he had considered administering to Kirkpatrick the thing that had proved fatal to the policeman. It had been patly at hand, as if he had known what he would find in the basement. But that would be explained by a telephone call to the nurse—was her name, Tarbell?—to have it ready for Kirkpatrick. He did not for a moment believe that Higgins, his own physician, and Kirkpatrick's, would have permitted use of the drug unless all other remedies had failed. Yet, before this, suspicion had pointed to Moreland as at least an ally of the poisoner....

Wentworth spoke abruptly, "I suppose you keep an alphabetical file of cases you handle, Dr. Moreland?"

The doctor frowned. The nurse moved to his side almost protectively, her blue eyes large on Wentworth's.

"Is there a reason for asking that?" Moreland demanded.

Wentworth nodded gravely, "And, doctor, does it include those patients who die under your treatments?"

Dark blood leaped to Moreland's cheeks. He stepped forward, his hands clenched, but the girl seized him with both hands. "Please, Tommy," she whispered, "can't you see he's goading you deliberately?"

"No," Wentworth still spoke gravely, deliberately, "I'm asking to obtain information." He drew from his pocket the paper which Kirkpatrick had left. "Are any of these persons, for instance, among your patients…?"

As Wentworth read the eighth name on the list, Moreland lifted a hand jerkily, but he waited until all had been called out before he spoke. "Miss Maitland," he said slowly. "I treated her for neuritis of the pectoral region. It apparently reached her heart…" He was frank, puzzled. His anger of a few moments

33

before had been soothed by the girl, by Wentworth's declaimer. "Just what are you getting at, Wentworth?"

Wentworth tapped the paper with his finger. "Commissioner Kirkpatrick believes that those people I named to you were poisoned. Dr. Hess' investigation confirmed that belief. I'm afraid, doctor, that I'll have to ask you to go with me to headquarters and make some explanations."

"You're inferring that I poisoned her!" Moreland cried hoarsely. "Why damn you, Wentworth…!" He tore from the girl's restraining hands, missed with a savage left and staggered back from a heart punch. Wentworth had stepped in, hit once with each fist, jumped past Moreland as he fell and seized the girl by the shoulders.

"You know about this!" he accused roughly. "You're the one who planted poison in the doctor's drugs!"

THE GIRL met his glare with a defiant fierceness, her chin lifted, color high in her cheeks. "You took a cowardly advantage of Tommy!" she cried, her accent broad. "And if you say either he or I poisoned Miss Maitland, then you're a liar!"

For a full half minute longer, Wentworth held the girl, staring into her eyes. They did not waver at all. He nodded abruptly, let her go.

"I believe in you and your faith, at least," he said.

She ignored him, kneeling by the doctor and massaging his neck with firm, competent fingers. Wentworth turned to Vanderveer.

"I think I'll be going," he said quietly. "I wonder if you'd be good enough to report to the police just what happened out there in the street."

"Rather!" Vanderveer cried, "But this bally beggar here? Aren't you going to turn him up to the bobbies?"

Wentworth shook his head. "Moreland can't get away," he said curtly. As he strode across the room, he thumbed fresh cartridges into partly emptied automatic clips. His frown lingered in his smoky eyes. He was still in grave doubt as to Moreland's innocence, but there was nothing yet to prove, even to the Spider, that he was guilty. And because the Spider waited not upon the processes of the law; because he was himself jury, judge and executioner, he must be completely sure of guilt before he struck. He told himself that he was not sure. In spite of cumulative evidence, he still felt an instinctive liking for Doctor Moreland. It proved nothing, of course, that the nurse, Tarbell, defended him. Fine women had before this become the slaves to infamy....

There was one more bit of investigation to be completed before he returned to his home: the garage across the street, from which the truck laden with beams had hurried. Before he went there, he strode toward his waiting taxi. The tail light had not been turned on with the coming of dusk, he saw, and though that did not necessarily indicate anything, Wentworth felt a slow coldness start up his spine. The pavement beside the parked taxi was empty, nor could he see any one through the back window. Wentworth's pace became almost a lope!

Beside the front seat, he paused, staring. It was empty. The rear… He yanked the door open and the ceiling light flicked on. A low cry squeezed from Wentworth's lips. The rear was not empty. The prisoner was gone, but the taxi driver was crumpled in a hideously distorted position on the floor. His face and hands, every visible inch of his flesh, was coated with coagulated blood which seemed to have oozed from the very pores. The eyes were sunken, the mouth twisted horribly.

Wentworth stepped back and stood sucking in deep, long breaths. No need to wonder what had happened here. The prisoner had—*poisoned*—his captor and escaped. Wentworth's face was rigid with shock and anger. He drew a notebook from his pocket with steady hands and wrote down the man's name and number. He, and no one else, was responsible for this man's death. The taxi driver had been performing a task allotted him by the Spider when he was killed. But, name of God, how could Wentworth have suspected that such horror threatened? He slapped the door shut, made a half turn so that he faced the garage. He went toward it with hard grinding heels.

The building was entirely deserted, and a policeman was in charge. The owner, he said, had not been located. It was a blind alley in his investigation. Wentworth swung lithely about and slapped his feet down hard while he hunted a cab. A pent-up impatience throbbed through his body. The enemy had been all about him, but he had failed in every instance to maintain contact. The policeman, faced with capture, had committed what amounted to suicide....

THE DRIVER of the taxi Wentworth hailed seemed to become infected with his impatience. He twisted about corners at reckless speed. He skidded the last ten feet to the doorway of Wentworth's apartment and a doorman sprang to the curb. He was a wide-shouldered husky with a long-barreled revolver at his waist.

He saluted as Wentworth stepped down, and he and another man formed a shield with their bodies. The lobby had a blind end with concealed gun slots; the elevator door was armored. This was Wentworth's own apartment building, his stronghold. He had found it wise to purchase the entire structure so that he could control tenancy and personnel and, after recent attacks, he had put armed men in all the corridors. For that reason, his building was chiefly occupied by wealthy men with valuable collections of one sort or another. They paid well for that armed retinue....

When the elevator reached the head of the shaft, the door had to be unlocked from the inside after due inspection through a peephole of bullet-proof glass. Wentworth stepped out and a man in a chauffeur's uniform that seemed almost military saluted briskly. His wide-jawed face split in a thin smile.

"Welcome home, Major!" he said cheerfully. "Miss Nita is inside."

Wentworth extended his hand and the two men shook firmly. "Glad to be back, Jackson, even if it does mean more fighting."

He nodded, went on into his penthouse apartment, and Jackson's eyes followed him loyally. They had been soldiers together in France, Sergeant Jackson and Major Wentworth, and each had saved the other's life a score of times here and abroad. Wentworth's old butler, Jenkyns, who had served his father before him, bowed deeply, wrinkled face wreathed in smiles as he took his master's hat.

"Welcome home, Master Dick!"

Wentworth was impatient to see Nita again. It had not been many hours since they had parted on shipboard, but so many things had happened since then. Here, in his home, was a fortress where she would be safe. Nita rose gracefully to meet him from a deep lounge-chair upon the terrace. He took her two slim hands and lifted each in turn to his lips, looked long into her eyes. It was an eternal miracle to him to discover always in their violet depths the love she bore so unwaveringly. She knew—she had known since that first day when he told her of the Spider's secret life—that they could never marry. How could the Spider permit himself a home and children when at any hour the hand of disgrace and death might fall upon his shoulder? Yet it had not turned Nita's love....

She drew him down beside her on a cushioned swing. Her voice was quiet and sweet, a bell-like contralto. "Do you want to tell me first what happened, or shall I talk about the ship's doctor?"

"You first," Wentworth said quietly. He sank back into the cushions and closed his eyes, her hands tight within his own. Almost, here under the stars, he could imagine peace and hope. Almost....

"I smuggled ashore the body of the monkey who stole the medicine the doctor gave you," Nita began…. The peace was gone. Wentworth saw again the white heat of the foredeck of the ship when the apparent attempt had been made on his life. He had gone to the doctor for a slight cold he had developed and, on the deck, had lain down in the sun to absorb its heat into his body. The medicine, still untouched, was in a box beneath his hand. He had been startled by a small furry hand snatching the box, had seen the monkey pet of a member of the crew skip across the deck and, chattering, swarm up a cargo boom mast forward. The monkey had taken the medicine, aping mankind, and he had died, writhing in agony; obviously poisoned. A few moments later, the doctor had rushed anxiously on deck, seeking Wentworth.

"I made a terrible mistake, Mr. Wentworth," he gasped, sweat streaming from his fiery red face. "I gave you…" He saw the dead monkey on the deck, the scattered pellets of the broken box. "Oh, thank God, Mr. Wentworth! Thank God!"

AT THE time, Wentworth had accepted the doctor's excuse at its face value. But later, when he began to think about the strange seizure of Kirkpatrick; when the other cases of poisoning had come to light in Kirkpatrick's list, he had wondered. It would have been so simple, that mistake in medicine; and the man the Underworld had for years fought vainly to remove would have been disposed of forever!

Nita described her movements in having an analysis to determine the kind of poison—the doctor, Heiman was his name—

had professed ignorance, saying that he had taken them from the body of a suicide.

"At quarantine," she said abruptly, "a private detective I recognized from the photographs in your files—Oscar Marsh—came to see Heiman. They were locked together in the doctor's office for half an hour—and Marsh left before the boat reached dock by the same launch on which he came.

Wentworth sat up sharply. "Marsh…?" He knew very little about the man. His reputation was not of the best, but there had been no serious charges against him. "I'll look him up," he decided grimly. He reached absently toward the nearby table where a box of chocolates reposed, handed them to Nita. As she took a chocolate, out of the French doors of the drawing-room romped a Great Dane dog. He bounded like a puppy, thrust his massive head into Wentworth's lap, tongue lolling, tail wagging, in a spasm of joy at seeing his master and mistress again.

"Ram Singh had him out," Nita said. "Want a chocolate, Apollo?" She popped the piece of candy into the dog's huge mouth. He swallowed it whole, then romped away, dashing in wide circles around the swing on which Wentworth sat, as if mere passive submission to caresses could not half express the joy of his welcome. He had made two circuits when he stopped. He skidded to a halt almost directly before them, stood rigid, every muscle braced, a whine in his throat.

Wentworth sprang to his feet. "What is it, Apollo?"

The dog wagged his tail faintly, looked toward Wentworth and fell writhing to the floor. The whine in his throat became a puppy whimpering. Convulsive shivers shook the huge body, the mouth yawned wide… and *he was dead!*

Wentworth stood rock-still, staring down at the lifeless bulk of the dog. Nita came dazedly to her feet, hand groping to Wentworth's arm, which almost violently enfolded her. Wentworth said, his voice stiff and harsh in his throat. "Poison! Somebody tried to poison us with that candy, and but for the accident of Apollo's eating a piece—but for Apollo…!"

Nita said, whispering: *"We would both be dead!"*

CHAPTER 4
WHEN DEATH WENT MAD!

INVESTIGATION REVEALED the poisoned candy had been in Nita's luggage when it arrived from shipboard. Jenkyns, in all innocence had placed it where she might find it. Wentworth telephoned the police to demand arrest of Dr. Heiman, aboard the *Transatlantica*, and was told that Heiman had been found, dead of poison, in his office shortly after the ship docked.

Wentworth and Nita stared at each other, bewildered at the news. Had the doctor honestly made a mistake and killed himself in remorse? Or had he failed in an appointed task and been murdered in retaliation?

"I think I'll have a talk with Oscar Marsh," Wentworth announced grimly. "He had an excellent chance to commit that murder… First, however, I'm going to pay a call to police headquarters. Ira Spangler is acting as commissioner in Kirkpatrick's place!"

Nita was grief-stricken over the gallant dog's death—he had been their strong support in many a battle—and Wentworth was no less shaken. But there could be no delay. The assassins of the poisoners had penetrated even into this stronghold. There was no way of telling how or where they would strike next….

Wentworth shook off his grief. "You remember Spangler, of course," he queried softly, almost as if he talked to himself. "I could never understand why Kirkpatrick appointed him. Effective enough in his work, probably. I don't trust him. The Underworld talks…."

Nita said slowly, "I remember a note in the files, that Spangler could be reached for protection. Costly, but could be had."

"That was just gossip, nevertheless… Nita—" Wentworth's voice grew stern—"You must not stir outside of this apartment!"

Nita moved toward him with small, quick steps, caught hold of his lapels. "Not… the Spider, Dick?" she whispered.

Wentworth laughed, but it was not a pleasant sound. "Do you think that Richard Wentworth, friend of Kirkpatrick, would have any influence over Spangler?"

"But Dick…!" Nita's voice died. She knew that the man she loved always chose the straight path to his purposes, that no fear of death or capture could swerve him from a chosen course. God knew that Dick risked death whenever he donned the black cape and sinister countenance of the Spider. At sight, any member of the Underworld would shoot to kill—mercilessly. Police might well do the same, for to them he was a murderer.

They did not consider that those he killed always richly deserved death. Yes, police undoubtedly would shoot the Spider on sight... Yet, unless Nita misunderstood his intention, Dick planned to invade police headquarters this night in the disguise of the Spider!

"Must you, Dick?" she whispered, and knew the answer even as she phrased it.

Wentworth's hands closed tightly on her shoulders; for a moment their lips clung together, then he went striding from her, crossed into his music-room and walked to where a great pipe organ filled an entire end of the room. Reaching high, he tapped rhythmically on the sound orifices of three pipes. The columns of air vibrated faintly, making a ghostly strain of music. Wentworth quitted them, walked along the paneled wall of the room and a secret door slid noiselessly aside. When he had stepped through, it closed again.

Beyond that paneled wall, Wentworth had a complete dressing-room with a hundred garbs and disguises. Hidden in a secret safe within that room was the disguise of the Spider, that fateful clothing whose mere possession would mean death to Wentworth were it found!

THESE THOUGHTS were far from his mind as he flung himself down before a dressing-table whose mirror was ringed with shielded neon lights. His deft fingers flew swiftly about their familiar task. Under their touch, a lotion tautened his skin so it shone across the cheekbones and became darkly sallow. Circles now appeared under his eyes, and his lips vanished, leaving his mouth a sinister, knife-thin line. That was all, except a reconstruction of the nose so that it became a hooked predatory beak, crowned by harsh, shaggy eyebrows, all topped by a lank, long wig, while the face that stared back at Wentworth bore no resemblance at all to the debonair countenance of Richard Wentworth, clubman, dilettante of the arts, and amateur criminologist. This was a face from whose glare the criminal guiltily shrank as from a death ray! This was the face of the Spider!

Rapidly, Wentworth donned a fresh suit of dark tweeds, a dark shirt that would not catch the gleam of light; then he drew down over his brows a black slouch hat, threw a long black cape about his shoulders. He stared at himself in the mirror, slowly twisted his shoulders so that they seemed distorted by some malignant disease. He limped heavily soundlessly, across the room. Yes, the Spider walked again....

The exit from the house was made smoothly. A second, hidden door that opened upon the service stairs, made the elevator available. A dark basement where the building superintendent did not watch too closely the entries and exits of the curious figures whom the night brought here. He believed that Richard Wentworth did secret police work, that these men who came and went—all of whom were Wentworth in disguise—were the myriad spies employed by the building's owner.

There was a private, single garage nearby and from it Wentworth drove a small, battered coupé whose engine was a match for the most powerful of modern machines…. The way to police headquarters was short; his means of entry uncomplicated. He stopped before the main door and emptied his automatic high through the front door so that no one would be hit. He doubled around the block, left the car in plain sight where it would not be suspected, and ducked into a back entrance, deserted now in the excitement at the street door. He knew this building as intimately as the palm of his hand. Up a back stairway, he crept to the hallway which led to the Commissioner's room. The commissioner himself, a thin, tall man with the stooped shoulder and gray face of a consumptive, stood in the doorway. Presently, an officer reported to him and Commissioner Spangler jerked a thin, long-fingered hand impatiently and turned back into his office. When the officer left, Wentworth slipped to the doorway. There was a single guard inside. Wentworth reached and felled him with a quick touch at certain throat nerve centers before the man could move. Easy to slouch him into a chair as if he slept, to palm open the door to the inner sanctum—the Commissioner's private office!

Wentworth eased through, stood with his shoulders resting lightly against the door. Spangler had not heard his entrance. He stood staring out the window. He cracked his knuckles with a slow violence that told of his tenseness. Wentworth eased forward, his mouth as harsh as the devil's judgment.

"Turn around, you cheap crook!" he said, raspingly.

Ira Spangler whirled about, his loose-jointed arms flinging wide. He lunged toward his desk where his revolver obviously lay, then he stopped, half-crouched over the desk, staring

DR. JOHNSON HESS

MAGDA HESS

VANDERVEER

into the big black eye of a heavy automatic in the Spider's hand. There were usually hectic spots of color high on his cheek-bones, but even those were gone leaving only the uniform, swarthy gray of his countenance.

WENTWORTH SMILED slightly and knew that it made the Spider's lips a sinister gash. "Touch no buttons, my dear Spangler, and no guns. I do not come to harm, but to instruct you!" He sent his flat, mocking laughter at the man and it seemed to accomplish what shock had not. Spangler went limp in every joint of his lank body and sprawled back in his chair. He wet his lips twice before he could speak.

"You didn't come to kill me, Spider!" he whispered. "You would have no reason to kill me. I'm the commissioner of the police! You are the friend of the police...."

"Strange to hear you say that now," Wentworth said quietly. "Quiet, let it pass... I have instructions for you. They are for the good of the city; for the benefit of the police."

Spangler still remained brokenly, now, sprawled in his chair. His long fingers moved restlessly on the arms. "Yes, yes," he whispered. "I'm always glad to learn things of benefit to...."

CAROLINE TARBELL

DR. MORELAND

THE DOCTOR

"It is simple," Wentworth interrupted. "Tonight, a member of the motorcycle police tried to kill Richard Wentworth. When the man was cornered, he took a drug that produced a catalepsis like death. It is very plain that, if he had not been killed his cataleptic body would have been stolen, his usefulness restored to the crook in whose employ he is. No, no, silence, Spangler!

The cure for this protection of the catalepsis drug is very simple. You will order your men to shoot to kill any prisoner seen taking such a drug, whether he bites it from his ring or takes a capsule. You will publicize that intention. I think it will put an end to such trickery on the part of the poison ring that is operating in the city."

Spangler licked his pale lips again. "I… I did not know about this… drug," he said heavily. "I think your idea is a good one, but I can't give such an order. Innocent people would be killed."

The Spider took a long stride forward "Innocent people have already been killed!" he grated. "Innocent people are being killed every day by these poisoners. You will issue those orders now, in my presence, and in the presence of newspaper men, or the Spider will replace you with someone who will be more amenable to suggestion. Do you understand, Spangler? In a file I have at my home, there is a notation that Spangler can be had for protection. It will cost money, this note says, but he can be bought. Yes, Spangler, I think you will do well to issue that order at once. But mind that you say only what I have instructed into that annunciator!"

Wentworth reached Spangler's side in long strides, passed him and stood upon the window sill. "Keep your eyes forward, Spangler! Remember my orders and see that you tell the newspaper men and your own force in full, or *I shall return!* I'll be listening while you talk!"

He edged out of the window, squeezing behind the edge of the jamb. Spangler lifted a bony hand to his forehead and dragged the palm hard across it. He wiped the palm on his blotter. When the door of his office opened and newspaper men flocked in, he did precisely as Wentworth had ordered.

"Aren't you the wisey, Spangler!" one of the reporters jeered. "How'd you figure out the catalepsis?"

Spangler sat more rigidly in his chair. "I have a tip from... the Spider," he said clearly. "A straight... red-hot... tip."

The reporters streaked for the door. Wentworth eased his grip on the bricks and toed back along the ledge to Spangler's window. "Very nice, Spangler," he jeered. "Very nice!" He sprang into the office and relieved Spangler of his gun. It would be easy to loop the light silk line he always carried about the radiator and slide out the window to the ground. He would wait, of course, until there was absolutely no chance for Spangler to cancel his previous statement....

OVER IN a corner of the room, the police news teletype came to life with an excited jangling of bells. Wentworth sprang to it, threw a glance at the jerking sheet of paper on which words were ticked out a letter at a time. Spangler, unchallenged, moved to where he could see and then the two men stared at each other with faces paling and eyes stretched wide.

"Homicide, Coney Island," the message ran. "Four people found poisoned and dead in amusement booth at Boone Park."

Spangler's phone rang shrilly and he stalked toward it, his ungainly figure covering space at surprising speed; Wentworth did not interfere. He listened while the acting commissioner rasped monosyllables at intervals. Presently, he slammed down the phone.

"I've got to get out of here," he said harshly. "Get to Boone Park."

Wentworth nodded jerkily, "What is it?"

"Seven more dead," Spangler barked. "It looks like wholesale murder!"

The Spider laughed and the sound was wild, furious. "Wholesale murder, yes, Spangler! And a murder master who will fill our city with corpses! Will you see to it, now, Spangler, that your men obey the shoot-to-kill order?"

Spangler made no answer, but sat with hunched shoulders at the desk, hands pushing down on its top. "Move," he insisted, "I've got to go!"

Wentworth nodded, made a loop about the radiator with his line and swung to the window sill. "If you so much as look out," he said, "you're going to lose the top of your head."

Twisting the light silken line which police called his "web" about his arms and leg, he slid rapidly downward. When he was twenty feet above the pavement, he felt the rope give and a sharp curse rose to his lips. Spangler was cutting his line! There was only one thing to do and Wentworth acted with the speed of instantaneous decision which had many times saved his life. He thrust both feet through a window he was passing, snatched at the frame. As toes and fingertips made the contact, the line gave way entirely and snaked toward him. For long seconds, Wentworth wavered on the brink of a fall which would have injured him severely, possibly killed him; then he caught his balance. He swayed forward into the room and was in a small office. A door in the opposite wall smacked open and two uniformed men came in behind their guns.

"Surrender, Spider!" they shouted. "You can't escape."

The two stood breathing heavily and behind them, echoing through the building, he could hear the deep harsh voice of Spangler, urging them on. "Shoot to kill!" he shouted. "The Spider...."

Wentworth had dropped behind the desk at the police challenge. He braced his shoulders against the wall, got his feet on the desk and thrust with every ounce of his strength. On protesting rollers, the desk shot toward the two policemen. One gun blasted, then the desk crashed into the two and hurled them to the floor. When they fell, Wentworth was already on his feet, bounding forward, and he hurdled the desk in a single stride, head pulled down to clear the doorway beyond. He smashed into another policeman, running to support the other two, and the blow hurled the man violently backward into a wall, dumped him unconscious on the floor.

The building was alive with racing, shouting men. Wentworth did the only possible thing. In a single bound, he was back at the entrance of the office he had fled. His return took the two floundering men by surprise and with two swift blows he laid them unconscious on the floor. He sailed his hat into the hallway, reached the window in a leap and swung out over the sill, dangling by his hands. His feet were almost fifteen feet from the pavement, but it was not an impossible leap. He pushed

out, dropped, lost his balance as his feet stung on the pavement. A bullet clipped the cement at his side, then he was crowding close to the building, racing at top speed for the corner. His ruse of indicating to the police that he had left the office by the door delayed the police there for seconds and undoubtedly saved his life. By the time they had discovered the trick and returned to the attack, he had rounded a corner and was sprinting toward his car. It leaped forward under his touch and he whirled it south.

People died up there—their bodies hurled from the cars by centrifugal force....

Two minutes later, his powerful though shabby car was roaring over Manhattan Bridge, headed for Brooklyn and Coney Island where Boone Park was situated....

THE CROWDED traffic of downtown Brooklyn fell behind him, the thinner blocks of residences. Presently, he became aware of a siren moaning off to his right somewhere and a while later another sounded on his left. An ambulance loomed out of the darkness behind and bellowed past, red headlights like bloodshot eyes. Wentworth's mouth tightened harshly as he swung in behind the speeding hospital car. There could be no doubt about the meaning of those sirens paralleling his own course to the Park. As he had feared when he made his dash from police headquarters, more deaths were being reported from Boone Park.

Ahead, down the length of the Avenue, Wentworth could already see the brilliantly lighted twin horns above the gates of Boone. A thickening stream of cars poured past him toward New York, machines weaving in and out with an almost frantic speed. One auto left the line and, taking the left hand lane of traffic with its horn blasting steadily, raced ahead with roaring motor. The ambulance swerved from its path. It almost scraped fenders with Wentworth. Other machines followed in its wake and the ambulance was crowded steadily closer to the curb. The accident happened without any warning at all.

One of the racing cars, a heavy sedan, jibbed from its course and headed straight for the ambulance. The hospital driver made a mighty effort and hurdled the curb. A light-post intervened, was smashed to earth in a blast of greenish light and the sedan ploughed into the wreckage. Wentworth barely braked to a halt in time, the nose of his coupé bumping lightly into the crumpled sedan. Through its broken windows, he could see the people within. Three men and two girls were there. One of the girls still lived. She was on the right in front and it was apparent that she had tried to take the wheel. Abruptly, as Wentworth watched, she reeled to her feet. The roof slammed her down, but she did not appear to notice. Her arms whipped about wildly, her head rolled, and a blueness crept over her face. When it reached her eyes, she made a final, convulsive leap and was still.

It had all happened so quickly! Wentworth was not out of his coupé when the girl gasped out her last breath. He stood staring into her strangled face, looked to the others in the sedan. All of them were like that, lips and faces dark with strangled blood. A great oath tore from Wentworth's mouth. Poisoned! There could be no doubt of it. These five had died of poison, the last of them being stricken at the wheel while he attempted to race the others to medical aid….

Wentworth flung himself back into the coupé, wrenched it clear and fought his way out into the stream of traffic and around the wreck. With throttle wide, he roared down the last stretch to the park. Even the panic stricken fugitives swept wide of his path, cars cringing almost like human things from the flare of his headlights. At the gates of the park, Wentworth jerked to a halt and flung out.

A cordon of police were ushering people from the gates as rapidly as possible, attempting to enforce a medical examination of each, but the thick stream of fleeing cars showed how vain was the effort. Wentworth slipped past the harassed men. Somewhere within this park, there must still be minions of the monster who had instigated the poisonings. If the poisons had not been administered recently, the deaths would have been detected sooner. But how to find the poisoners among this fleeing stream? They would know their part. They would be the most frightened among all this panicky crowd....

THE CONTAGION of fear was widespread, but it had not yet affected all of the people, by a wide margin. Wentworth's eyes narrowed as he saw that several food and confection booths within his sight had not been closed; in fact were thronged with people. Why, damn it, what was being handed out now might well contain the germs of death! With long strides, Wentworth reached the nearest of the booths, wrenched his way through the jammed customers, and leaped to the counter.

"Fools!" he shouted. "This food may be poisoned! Don't you know that a dozen people have been found dead here tonight, poisoned by something eaten at the park?"

The people stared at him white-faced. A man behind the counter came rolling toward him angrily. "What are you talking about?" he demanded. "Trying to ruin my trade?"

Wentworth turned his head and looked down at the man and he stopped, staring, his mouth open, into the leanly stern face of the Spider.

"You will close this booth," Wentworth directed quietly. 'That is an order!"

The man cringed back. "The Spider," he whispered. "It's the Spider..." He turned and ran, scrambled over a counter and ran, screaming. His fear spread. Everywhere people turned and fled. Another man behind the counter jerked his hand out from a box and leveled a revolver. Before he could fire, Wentworth's hand had whipped an automatic out and a bullet was through the man's wrist. One of the poisoners? Wentworth sprang toward him. The man cringed back, abruptly slapped a hand to his mouth. Wentworth knew that gesture….

Deliberately, as the man slumped to the floor under the cataleptic drug he had taken, Wentworth shot him through the heart. He would spread the fear of death among the followers of the poisoner! When they learned that their cataleptic drug no longer saved them from the wrath of justice… Wentworth did not delay. He saw a policeman struggling through the fleeing crowds toward him and dodged into a dark by-way. Damn it, why hadn't the booths been closed at once on the arrival of the police? It was the obvious source of death, yet this simple precaution had not been taken.

Wentworth raced toward another booth and shouted his warning. The man behind the counter at this place merely laughed.

"Aw, what's eating the nut?" he demanded. "Seen a ghost, fellah?"

There were giggles in the crowd. Wentworth whirled angrily on the operator of the stand and, in turning, his eyes flashed beyond him toward one of the amusement devices called the "Old Mill." Boats propelled by a moving current of water traveled through dark tunnels along which there were lighted "views." It was chiefly occupied by spooning couples and the boat that was just coming out of the darkness into light held two such pairs of girls and men. On their faces was none of the usual laughing confusion of the young lovers. Their faces were blue, and they lolled in the clutch of death! Wentworth pointed a violent hand at the bodies!

"Eat then!" he cried. "Eat, and die with the blue death blush upon your faces!"

A woman screamed and men, staring where he pointed, turned gray. The operator of the booth gabbled unintelligibly and when Wentworth again ordered him to close he nodded an eager assent and Wentworth dashed on about his task. On the main midway, he met a stampede of human beings which almost knocked him from his feet. He worked his way to one side of the wide amusement street and pushed on. The screams of women and the angry cries of men sounded above the jangle of carnival music, above the mechanical clatter of amusement devices....

The rush and the roar of a nearby switchback pulled his eyes in that direction and, abruptly, he understood the reason for the panic. From the darkness which shrouded the crest of the swooping, curving tracks of the roller coaster, a dark object hurtled into sight. It was followed by a second and a third. The objects flew out into the midst of the crowd and, as they swooped into the brilliance of the lights, Wentworth could see that arms and legs dangled brokenly from them. They were human bodies! WHEN THEY crashed into the ranks of the crowd, absolute terror swept over the close-packed way. A woman with a child in her arms was rushed along with the stampede, struggling only to keep her feet. She was twenty feet from Wentworth when she went down and the crowd closed over her. Wentworth charged to her aid, head and shoulders and voice fighting to open a path. It seemed hours before he reached her and snatched her to her feet. He drifted with the crowd then, working his way slowly to one side. The woman babbled incoherent thanks, clasping the child tightly in her arms. They reached the protection of a booth that thrust into the crowd and the woman looked down at her child. She screamed then. As she fled again, carrying her child in her arms, Wentworth saw that someone had stepped on the child....

There was no use trying to stem the panic, even if that were possible. The people were dashing from the park and in that lay their greatest hope of survival. Easy to understand what had happened to catapult these corpses into the crowd. It was plain that the poison was one which affected the heart. The blueness of the faces and the appearance of strangulation proved that. It might be *digitalis* which, in excessive doses, causes extreme dilation of the heart. The gasping dive of the switchback would consummate the effects of the drug and the inert bodies had been hurled from the cars by centrifugal force....

Deliberately, Wentworth spread the panic. It would act swifter than the closing of the booths could. He rushed scream-ing through quiet crowds, shouting wild things about death and murder. He staged a false hold-up and sent his humming lead high over the heads of the people. He set fire to a small and isolated booth. Sometimes the mere glimpse of his becapped figure was enough, but he kept on the pressure. It was exhaust-ing, dangerous work. Always there was the chance that, in exposing himself, he might be seen by an armed policeman or emissary of the poisoners. A single well-placed bullet was all that was needed to end any man's life....

But he escaped that peril, and presently the last of the crowd was streaming through the gates of the park. Wentworth did not leave at once, though his work was done here as much as ever it might be. Through the darkened and tawdry lanes of the amusement center, he made his way back toward that first booth where he had shot down a man who undoubtedly was a minion of the poisoners. The booth was still open, its counters stripped and Wentworth glided inside, found the dead man. His most rigorous search revealed only one thing, a slip of paper that read: *"Dock Guard."*

There was no explanation, no number of a pier, just those two words and the Spider, crouched in the darkness, stared fiercely before him. He felt abruptly certain that here was a hint of some more awful crime. It might, of course, mean merely that the man was to guard some private dock of the poisoners, but impatiently, Wentworth thrust aside that explanation. If this were a mere designation to routine duty, it would not have been necessary to give written instructions. More probably, it designated his part in some new series of murders, and a dock meant... a ship, a passenger steamer!

Wentworth's curse rasped in his throat. There was nothing in the world more terrible than death and panic at sea. No man who had not lived through such horror could realize the transcendent dread of being trapped on the narrow confines of a ship and knowing that death was rampant, that it might strike in the next instant anywhere—and that there was no escape! DOWN ON his knees again beside the corpse, Wentworth once more made a frantic search, but nowhere on the body was there any further hint as to what dock, hence what ship, was designated. God, he must find out, he *must*....

But how? There was no way save to find the poisoner, or more of his men, and force the truth from them. And there was no help here....

The park was empty now, booths closed and dark. It was easy to slip away into the shadows and make his way to the waiting car. The Spider, with the more conspicuous items of his disguise laid aside, drove swiftly back to New York. A furious necessity for action racked him, and in the back of his mind was the constant picture of those who had died back there in the park. He had seen half a hundred bodies strewn on the ground and in the various buildings, covered each with its pitiful coarse shroud of canvas. When even that poor covering failed, hats and coats had been used. But for the Spider's prompt action, the carnage might have been even more fearful, but that was poor consolation. Until he could find and destroy the poisoner himself, such scenes would continue. And a ship was next....

An idea struck Wentworth and he slammed the car to the curb. There could be no reasonable doubt that the poisonings were either the work of a madman, or had been committed for profit. Madmen did not gather gangs of men together and place their hirelings on the police force. So... murder for profit. It wouldn't take much inquiry to learn who would profit most by the closing of Boone Park. Had not McCloskey, the political boss who owned most of the Coney Island section, attempted to purchase Boone?"

McCloskey's reputation was well known to Wentworth. There had never been any direct evidence against the man, but more than once there had been indications of criminal tie-ups, of cooperation with gangsters. If the Spider paid him a call... McCloskey might be difficult to locate, but a phone call... He stripped off his disguise, sought a phone. Wentworth was disappointed. McCloskey was in the Bahamas and had been for two weeks, he and his friend, Kennesaw Ives.

Wentworth bit his lips, stood drumming on the phone-booth wall with his fingertips. Of course, McCloskey's absence did not disprove his guilt. It merely made conviction more difficult, and... With an abrupt tightening of his eyes, Wentworth called a newspaper acquaintance and began a checkup of other possible poisoning cases of which he knew. It was a coincidence that of the eleven on the list, the chief beneficiary in each case had been out of the city at the time of the tragedy....

"WHAT'S UP, Mr. Wentworth?" the reporter inquired. "You think there was something phony about those deaths? Funny that in each case, the beneficiary had built an alibi."

"Funny, yes," Wentworth said quietly, "but you can't cast suspicion on those people without more basis than I have." His eyes narrowed, staring at the side of the phone-booth. "Why not play it this way? Why not, when the next similar death is reported, with the beneficiary away, tip off police anonymously to give that beneficiary a tossing around?"

"Swell!" the reporter cried. "Swell... Listen, here's something right now. Here are three cases tonight in which whole families were wiped out by poison. Whole families with, in each case, one exception!"

Wentworth felt tenseness creep into his body. A story to the newspaper man, the deaths of all those families—just headline material....

ENTIRE FAMILY DIES;
POISON IS SUSPECTED AFTER SEVEN PERISH!

Sure, fine headline material. A grandmother's white head had sagged in death, her daughter and son-in-law, whose hand had been lifted from the control of a company which vitally needed his steady guidance. A brother, three children on the threshold of adult life. They had sat down to a dinner table of gleaming crystal and white linen. Which of them could know that the seeds of death lurked in their savory food? And who had survived...? The son of the father by a first marriage. He would succeed to the control of the business, to all the wealth built by two generations of strenuous effort. That son....

"Went to Chicago on business a week ago," the reporter replied quickly. "Say, do you think he had a hand in it? He's flying back, ought to hit the Newark Airport in a couple of hours."

Wentworth's mouth curved in a harsh smile. "No, I don't think Charlie Skeer had anything to do with it. I know him, and he's not the type. It must be an accident this time. No, I don't think I'd tip off the police about him...."

63

Wentworth left the phone-booth and reached his car with long striding haste. He didn't want the police to seize Skeer—not yet. But there would be an unexpected welcoming committee at the Newark airport when Skeer landed, a committee of one for justice—the Spider! But he would have to work fast, fast if he were to save the doomed souls on whatever ship was sailing this night with death in her hold!

The Spider was soaring over Manhattan bridge when the idea struck him with the violence of a bullet—men who stood to profit by these wholesale poisonings invariably were away when they were committed; a ship was to be attacked tonight... and Kennesaw Ives, who was away with McCloskey in the Bahamas, was president of a ship line! If there was one of the rival line sailing tonight....

It took Wentworth precious minutes to reach a telephone, more precious moments to locate the office of Ives' line, then he slammed up the receiver and stood with clenched fists, jaw knotted in futile anger. The Harper liner, S. S. *Kendall* had sailed two hours before for Cuba, with a passenger list of one thousand souls!

CHAPTER 5
DOOM SHIP

WENTWORTH MOVED slowly again to his car. He could overtake the S. S. *Kendall* in a seaplane in less than an hour, but once aboard, it might take him long to discover whether his suspicions concerning her were correct and mean-

LABORATORY OF THE DAMNED

time… meantime, if he were wrong, the poisoners would already have struck! He felt a high, mounting tension in his breast, but mechanically he went about making arrangements. There was no other course. The captain would not heed a radio message from anyone less than the owner, and how could he persuade even so bitter a competitor as the Harper concern that Ives would descend to murder? And there was no time, no time…!

His orders to Nita van Sloan were staccato and gave no evidence of the doubts that shook him: His seaplane to the Battery dock at once, Jackson to Newark airport to follow Skeer. Jackson was to watch for any suspicious contacts which young Skeer might make with crooks. When those orders had been relayed, he had a moment for Nita. Swiftly, he narrated what had happened, his suspicions of Ives and about the *S. S. Kendall.*

"You're going aboard the *Kendall,* Dick?" Nita asked quietly.

"I have no choice," Wentworth told her rapidly. "Nita… can you come to the dock?"

Nita's voice came back crisply. "I can do better than that. I'm going with you, and don't try to argue, Dick, lover."

She hung up lest her instructions go unheeded and Wentworth hurried to the car again with a wistful smile on his lips. There had been a haunting, but still unphrased fear in Nita's heart through the long months of struggle, a fear that kept her close at his side in the thick of deadly peril. Any farewell of theirs might be the last this side of the grave, and Nita was determined that if death should overtake her lover in the pursuit of his self-imposed task of administering his swift justice, it should find her by his side. How could he deny her that, he who must deny her so many things that must be the dream of every woman?

So when Nita reached the dock, she found not the protest she had expected, but the tender arms of her lover. Wentworth smiled down at her, and who can blame him if his eyes shone with moisture that was almost tears?

"I'm not going to argue, beloved," he whispered.

The plane hummed out of the eastern sky and skimmed to the water in the track of the Statue of Liberty's light, then taxied, roaring, across the Harbor. A crowd seeking the cool of the Battery Park crowded against the sea-wall to watch the craft skim close, stared curiously at the man and woman who took over the ship from the airport attendant, who saluted Wentworth by name.

His name ran in a shrill whisper through the crowd. They knew this man and his exploits under his own identity. If they had known that other fearful name, the Spider... But they didn't. A ragged cheer lifted as Wentworth gunned the motor experimentally, and he swung a hand in farewell, lifted the plane skillfully from the black waters. Nita sat beside him in the forward cockpit, the attendant alone behind. It was necessary to take him, for he must follow the ship when Wentworth had gone aboard, and if he were wrong in his guess, if the *Kendall* was not the doomed ship... Well, he must race back to try again. Only, he knew there would be no second chance. If he failed this time, it would be... too late!

The charm of the night seascape below, of the girl beside him could mean little to him tonight. Death lay ahead, not alone for

these two, but perhaps for the thousand aboard the *Kendall*...
Then miles off Sandy Hook, Wentworth picked up the lights of
a ship and, at his instructions, Nita began to call the *Kendall*, as if
they were two late passengers for the cruise. Would the *Kendall*
stand by? Two late passengers who would try to avert the visit
of a third and unwanted visitor... Death himself!

THEY MADE the contact, taxied along-side and the airport
attendant stared wide-eyed at Wentworth's instructions.

"You mean you want me to just stay here and every now and
then hop up to near the ship?" he asked, aghast.

Wentworth smiled at him. He drew out a checkbook and
scribbled in it rapidly in his clear, vigorous writing and the man's
expression turned to a wide smile.

"Hell, Mr. Wentworth," he muttered, "Beg your pardon, lady,
but this is too much, sir. A thousand dollars...."

Wentworth was already out on the wing, hands lifted to help
Nita from the cockpit. For a moment he held her close in his
arms, then they scrambled up the accommodation ladder and
the impatient *Kendall* was immediately on her way with a deep
blast of her whistle. The plane wheeled away, skimmed from the
water and vanished into the night. Wentworth forced his lips to
smile as a junior officer greeted them. He hoped he would not
be recognized, for he had no way of telling whether even this
officer might be one of the poisoners!

"Take us to your captain at once," Wentworth instructed
the man.

"The captain's on the bridge, sir," the officer said courteously,
"I am empowered to take care of you in every detail."

Wentworth shrugged. "Very well." Best not to arouse suspicions. There were too many curious faces about, too many intent eyes. Nita touched his arm, "I'll make the arrangements, Dick," she said. "You can look up Mr. Roberts right away."

Wentworth gratefully accepted the lead Nita had given him and strode off along the decks, made his way straight for the bridge. He glanced back once and saw that Nita had wholly engaged the attention of the junior officer… Captain McRae met Wentworth with a stiff-necked and belligerent pose. "Passengers are allowed on this bridge only by invitation," he said stiffly. "I'll ask you to remove yourself." Wentworth bowed suavely. "I hope you'll pardon the intrusion," he said, "the truth is…" He hesitated, meeting the glowering regard of the old Scot. How to convince this man on the flimsy evidence which he had that the food of his ship was poisoned, if indeed that was the case. He was aware of a footstep behind him.

"Mr. Mate," came McRae's voice sharply, "Escort this passenger from the bridge!"

Wentworth swung about and the mate winked at him very circumspectly. "Yes, Captain," said the mate. "Would you mind, sir?"

Wentworth liked the man instantly, the merry way his blue eyes sat in his wind-burnt face, the crispness of his speech and movements. He swung about and bowed to the captain. "I wished to thank you for your courtesy in stopping for us," he said, then he stalked away from the indignant captain with the younger mate.

"My name is Holcomb," the mate introduced himself, "I'm

sure you won't take offense at Captain McRae, and it is a violation of rules, you know."

Wentworth faced him in the starboard corridor. He began to talk rapidly, "Don't take me for a maniac right away, Mr. Holcomb," he said, "but do you remember the poisonings that have been reported in New York recently? Did you hear of the outbreak at Coney Island tonight?"

The mate stared at him curiously, a speculative light in his blue eyes, but he nodded.

Wentworth met his stare very directly, "I have reason to think that the food on this ship may have been poisoned by the same men who killed those other people," he said. "It's scanty reason, I admit in advance, but I don't believe that any chance should be taken, do you?"

The mate smiled slightly, "You expect me seriously to believe, sir…?"

WENTWORTH THREW up his hands. It was always this way. It was one of the reasons why the Spider had been born, the utter inability of people to believe the incredible ferocity of criminals, the wide scope of their activities. It would be simple to make tests of the food. There must be some animals on the ship, or a doctor who would have chemicals, but the mate would not even take the necessary precaution… It was getting well on into the morning. Dawn had broken while the plane winged to sea and within an hour at most, the breakfast gong would ring….

"Holcomb," he said urgently, "what possible harm can tests of the food cause? Wouldn't you take that step to make sure?"

Holcomb hesitated, looked down at the deck. He shook his

head. "I'll be quite frank," he said. "You're a man I'm inclined to trust and believe, but I couldn't take such a step without the captain's consent. It might alarm the passengers...."

"Damn it, man, would you rather *kill* the passengers?"

"I really don't have the authority, sir," Holcomb said, "but if you'll come back with me to see the captain...."

Wentworth nodded slowly, but he knew in advance the futility of argument with McRae. To be sure, he could force his way into the kitchens behind a gun, but it would be almost impossible to make tests of the food after that. He would be immediately suspected, since he had mentioned it to Holcomb... And, damn it, minutes were precious. If this were the wrong ship, it would be impossible now to race back to New York, to find the right one. His lips thinned and his right hand moved more swiftly than the eye could follow. When it reappeared, it held a gun close against Holcomb's side.

"Believe me," Wentworth said swiftly, "the tests are necessary and you know as well as I that McRae can't be convinced. We are going to test that food."

Holcomb's eyes flashed with rage and for a moment it was plain he hesitated on the verge of resistance, but something he saw in Wentworth's gaze seemed to convince him of its futility. He shrugged slightly.

"It's your deal, sir," he said, "and you'd better fill your hand pat. This will be classed as piracy in the federal courts."

"We'll go to the kitchens," Wentworth repeated. "I'm sorry about this, but it's necessary. Lead on, and don't attempt trickery."

They went to the kitchens. A score of stewards and cooks were seated about long tables eating. Wentworth stood close to Holcomb in the doorway.

"Ask for the menu," he ordered softly, "then for samples of all the foods to be placed on a tray and taken to your cabin."

Holcomb obeyed and Wentworth watched the men in the kitchen closely. The order was obeyed without question nor could Wentworth detect any signs of alarm among the kitchen workers. Was it possible that, after all, he was mistaken? Had he misread the entire purport of that note in the poisoner's pocket? He reminded himself that the poisoners would not necessarily be among the kitchen force, that indeed he would make every effort not to be in the kitchen since its workers would be the first to fall under suspicion....

"We'll go to your cabin now," Wentworth directed Holcomb, and the officer obediently stepped back out of the kitchen and led the way along a corridor.

"I'M AFRAID you're all wet on this," Holcomb said quietly, "if you're telling the truth about what you think. I watched those birds in the kitchen and not one of them was scared. I don't think..." He broke off, his voice ending in an oath as a man's choked scream rang out behind them. Wentworth whirled and together, the two raced back toward the kitchen. They found the man who had screamed writhing on the floor of the corridor. There was a knife hilt protruding between his shoulders and a tray of food was smashed over the deck. Frightened faces of men peered from the kitchen door and Holcomb shooed them back. Wentworth had holstered his gun and the two men met each other's eyes grimly. Wentworth nodded, stooped over the knifed man who now was dead and rolled him over on his back. From between his lips protruded a fragment of bread and, distinctly to their nostrils, came the odor of burnt almonds....

"You can't mistake it;" Wentworth said triumphantly, "That odor means cyanide of potassium!"

Holcomb uttered an exclamation and dropped upon his knees. Wentworth heard a quick, light footstep behind him and whirled. He was in time to dodge the knife thrust of the man just behind him, but that was all. Before he could utter more than a startled cry five other men burst from the kitchen door and overwhelmed him. He carried the knife man down with him, hands gouging into his throat. He heard Holcomb curse, then something crashed lightning into his skull and he slid down a steep incline into unconsciousness....

IT WAS Nita's urgent voice which called him back from the painful depths to full consciousness, but his will seemed sluggish. Finally, he fought back and opened his eyes.

"Oh, thank God," he heard Nita whisper. "Thank God! Dick, lover, the breakfast gong just rang!"

For a moment those words made no sense at all; then Wentworth thrust upward from the floor on which he lay. He realized that on Nita's head was the broad black hat that the Spider wore and across her shoulders the long cape....

"I frightened them away from you and the mate with these," Nita explained rapidly. They were going to kill you, but they thought I was the Spider..." She laughed, and there was a shrill edge to her voice. "I'm afraid the mate is dead."

Wentworth's head was reeling dizzily and there was a pain that blurred his thoughts, but he reached for the hat and cape as Nita spoke. He stood for a moment staring down at Holcomb, whose chest was covered with blood, whose head lolled loosely on his shoulders. He shook his own head violently and almost fell with the pain. He dragged the black hat down on his temples, improvised a mask with a handkerchief.

"Lucky you brought these things," he muttered, "I thought you had clothing for yourself in that grip." He staggered to the door, but Nita sprang in front of him and set her hands against his chest.

"Wait a minute, Dick," she whispered, "just a little minute until you've recovered fully."

He stood there, panting, sucking in deep breaths, fighting for clarity against the pain and dazzle in his brain. Finally, he smiled and nodded slightly.

"All right now, dear," he said. "Keep in the background, and don't do anything regardless of what happens."

Nita clung to him for a moment. She knew what he meant, that to help the Spider would not only brand her as an accomplice, but it would identify them both despite the Spider's garb and disguise… She backed away and put her hands behind her, smiling bravely into his eyes, and Wentworth gazed on her for a moment and was gone, sliding silently along the corridor. It was always thus that she sent him into battle, with a brave smile… The ache was still in his brain, but it was subordinate to the swift procession of his thoughts. There was no question now that he was on the right ship, the poisoning of the steward who had greedily helped himself from the tray of food being borne to Holcomb's quarters, the attack proved that past any question. He knew also that he had to deal with many enemies, and that he would not be able to convince the passengers of the horror that threatened. He would have to frighten them into obedience, or else… but there was no alternative. If he failed in this attempt….

A WOMAN came abruptly out of a stateroom door, stared at him and jumped back inside with a muffled scream. Wentworth could hear the lock and bolts snap shut, heard the buzz of the steward's signal as she summoned help. He increased his pace. The dining salon was well aft on a lower deck. A man saw his becapped, twisted form and began to run, feet slapping frantically. There was no further use in secrecy. Wentworth ran after him, spun down a companion-way and sprang between groups of holiday passengers into the door of the salon itself. He leaped to a table and threw up his hands, a gun clenched tight in each fist.

Men and startled women whirled toward him. A steward ducked behind the screen that hid the kitchen doors. For a moment, Wentworth said nothing. He sent the low, mocking laughter of the Spider over the crowded dining-salon.

"The Spider!" a woman screamed. "The Spi-i-ider!" She fainted and, slumping against a man, carried him with her to the floor.

"Yes, the Spider!" Wentworth shouted, his voice flat and rasping. "Let not a man move! Ladies and gentlemen, I bring you a warning! This food is poisoned. Let no man or woman eat of it lest he die!"

A junior officer came from behind the kitchen screen and walked very deliberately forward across the room.

"This is nonsense," he said sharply. "Get down off that table, Spider."

Wentworth's right hand gun blasted and the bullet bored a hole in the deck at the officer's feet He stopped, his face paling. Men were on their feet everywhere, muttering.

"You're just trying to create a panic," the officer said, resolutely. "It's foolish to say that the ship's food is poisoned!"

"The food is poisoned!" Wentworth thundered. "Haven't you heard how they died in New York? How scores of people fell dead at Coney Island, poisoned by the very food that brought them pleasure…?" But he was failing. It was plain that no one believed him, and it was only a question of time before an officer shot him from the table, or one of the poisoners struck….

"Nonsense," the officer cried. "You are just spreading panic There is a penalty for that Spider, and…."

A woman's scream cut him short. A woman sprang to her feet from a table and stood rigidly, both arms thrust above her head, mouth and eyes wide. It was Nita! For a moment Wentworth had a mad thought that she had been poisoned, and then he perceived how cleverly she had disobeyed his injunction. She had slipped into the dining salon behind him and now she was faking a poisoning…. Even as Wentworth realized her purpose, Nita flung herself to the floor and writhed there as if in the last throes of convulsive death.

"See!" Wentworth shouted. "Already the poison strikes! Already death is among you. Death is in your food…."

"The woman is faking," a voice said calmly from behind Wentworth. "Get down off that table, before I blow your head off!"

Wentworth came down from the table, but not as the speaker had intended. He came down in a backward somersault that sent him crashing into the man who had challenged him, another officer of the ship. But the damage had been done. Other ship's men were charging in on him from all sides, and from the kitchen there burst a score of men in stewards' and cooks' uniforms whom Wentworth had reason to believe were the allies of the poisoners!

THE SPIDER could have checked that pursuit with a half-dozen bullets placed with an accuracy that only he could achieve, but he could not know which were killers and which honestly thought him a danger to the ship's safety. There was nothing to do save flee and he did that with astonishing speed. His somersault landed him on his feet, though staggering from collision with the man who had challenged him. He let the stagger carry him backward, speared a column with his left arm, swung about it and was bolting up the companion at top speed. A dozen strides along a corridor brought him to a companionway. It was the work of seconds then to doff hat, cape and mask and thrust them into a ventilator. It would have been easier to throw them into the sea, but he was by no means sure that the battle was won.

Within a half hour, his forethought was proved wise. The passengers were completely persuaded that it was a gigantic hoax of some kind and a few who partook of food were unharmed. The damnable cleverness of it! Wentworth had no illusions about the success of his effort. The criminals could not leave off their plans now. They were encouraging the mass of the passengers to eat by letting the courageous few go unharmed. When the room was full again… Wentworth faced Nita grimly in the stateroom which had been allotted to them. Nita's face was very pale.

"They've found Holcomb," she said. "He's in the sick bay. If he recovers consciousness and tells them what you said, they'll come for you. They'll know you're the Spider."

Wentworth shrugged. Such peril was constant. But what could he do to avert the death that reached out even now for the passengers of the ship? At any moment, the crooks might begin serving the poisoned food and there was no chance that he would be able to invade the kitchen. Armed men had been placed at the portals by the captain. Poor fool, didn't he know that the danger was already within? There was a desperate gleam in Wentworth's eyes.

"There's only one chance left, Nita," he said abruptly. "We aren't far from shore. Take a life preserver, Nita, and go on deck."

Nita ran to him, caught his shoulders, "What, Dick?" she whispered. "Oh, what are you going to do?"

Wentworth's lips were grim. "This is an American boat," he said. "Thanks to the recent clean-up, they'll have efficient sailors. There probably won't be any loss of life in an emergency. If the poison is fed to the passengers, they'll die in droves…" He sucked in a deep breath. "I'm going to set the ship on fire!"

For a moment Nita thought to protest, then she stepped away

from him and met his gaze directly. "You are right," she agreed quietly. "It is the only way. Can't I help?"

"Go on deck," Wentworth told her briskly, "and hurry. Every second is precious. At any moment, the poison…" Nita fled, and Wentworth ran through the corridors and snatched hat and cap again. In a cabin near the dining salon, he piled bed clothes and folding chairs in the middle of the floor and torched them with a twisted bit of paper. He streaked down a companionway and started another fire on the deck below, raced forward toward the cargo hold. Within three minutes, he had started fires in a half-dozen places. But they must not be discovered too quickly. A fire-alarm would stampede the passengers from the dining salon, but….

Wentworth's breath came sharply. He rushed at frantic speed, setting more fires and finally, he smashed a glass panel in a corridor and jerked the hook of the fire alarm. Instantly, the siren of the ship began to bellow, bells jangled everywhere. A junior officer pounded along the corridor at a hard run, hut went on past the cabin where the Spider crouched. Wentworth raced behind him toward the dining-salon and frightened men and women fled from his path. It took only moments to find the liquor supply, to smash bottles and toss a lighted match into the alcohol. Instantly, the blue spirit flames were everywhere.

STILL, THE Spider's work was not done. The passengers, in the present situation, would be assembled on deck ready to abandon ship, but not unless the fire broke beyond control, or all chance of reaching shore was lost would Captain McRae give the order to take to the boats. Wentworth must make sure that the fire was not put out too quickly. He must lurk in the vicinity of the blaze, cut hose-lines, drive back fire-fighters… It was dangerous work, but presently the Spider had succeeded in fanning the blaze in the dining-salon beyond all possibility of control. It had broken through into the kitchen, to the deck above and adjoining salons and cabins were afire. Then, and not until then, did Wentworth desert the smoke-choked passage-ways and, face muffled in his cloak, make his way laboriously to the deck. Nita was instantly beside him.

"The captain is searching the ship for you, Dick," she whispered urgently. "He won't give the order to abandon ship. See?"

Wentworth looked where she pointed and saw McRae, a revolver in each fist, backed by junior officers and crew, holding back people from the boats.

"We're in no danger," McRae thundered, "I'll shoot the first man that makes a break for the boat!"

Wentworth leaned his shoulders against the bulkhead, breathing deeply. He coughed rackingly now and again from the smoke fumes.

"They've got to take to the boats," he said quietly. "I'll go to the deck above and take McRae from behind. You lead the rush for the boats when I overpower him."

Nita's hand lingered on his arm for a moment, then she walked away along the deck toward McRae without another word. Wentworth sprang to his new task with fresh vigor. McRae had chosen a good spot from his viewpoint, blocking the companionway that led upward to the boat-deck. But it made it an easy matter to get behind him, provided Wentworth could reach the boat-deck. He reached the bulkhead beside a companionway aft and checked, listening. He could hear the murmur of two men's voices, the guard. Wentworth's guns flipped to his hands. He stepped quietly before the two men and while they still stared at him, he reached out and struck them both unconscious to the deck. They would not be out long, since he had hit lightly, but long enough for him to accomplish his purpose.

On the boat deck, he did not hesitate, but sprinted toward the steps that McRae guarded. For a moment he crouched at their head, then launched himself in a long, diving tackle toward the braced back of the captain. A man shouted. A woman hid her face in clutching hands, then Wentworth's full weight struck McRae on the shoulders and the two lunged to the deck. The Spider balled, somersaulted and landed running on his feet, took out a junior officer with a neat left and right to the jaw.

"To the boats!" he shouted. "The ship is burning!"

Nita echoed his cry shrilly, "To the boats!" She led the scramble toward the steps. Wentworth stood alertly, guns covering the officers and members of the crew on guard.

"Easy!" he cautioned the people. "There's plenty of time. Take it easy." He laughed. "Anybody would think it was rush hour in the subway!"

A few men stared at him pale-faced, then one of them smiled a little. The panic slowed… and Wentworth saw McRae. The captain had eased up on an elbow and his revolver was leveled at Nita, just reaching the head of the steps. With an oath the Spider fired. The bullet slapped the man's gun from his hand and McRae slumped back to the deck. Wentworth was instantly on guard again, but it was too late. Officers and men were upon him in a single, mad leap and he was crushed under their numbers, disarmed, held helpless to the deck.

DESPAIR FLASHED through Wentworth's heart. In a few moments, McRae would recover consciousness and, with his stubborn refusal to abandon ship, doom the thousand people whom Wentworth had risked so much to save. It was that more than his own fate; if he failed to escape, which concerned the Spider in that moment.

"You fools!" he cried, his voice strangled. "The ship is doomed! Escape while there is time!"

He knew the futility of trying to persuade these men, of seeking to influence McRae....

"Let that man up!" The voice, somewhere near, was weak, but utterly confident. "Let the man up. McRae is out of this and I'm captain now. Move...." A shot cracked out. A man yelped, but in fright, not pain. The crushing weight of the men on top of Wentworth lifted a little and presently he could see Holcomb, bracing himself against a stanchion, chest bandage stained with blood, a gun in his right hand. Holcomb smiled a little, his face white. There was still blazing life in his blue eyes.

"Mr. Carson," he said clearly, "Prepare to abandon ship. The fire is out of control."

Wentworth got stiffly to his feet. Fortunately, the mask was still over his face. He caught up his hat and guns from the deck and crossed to Holcomb's side to help him. He disguised his voice.

"I'm glad one of the officers has retained his sanity," he said pleasantly. "I'm afraid McRae will recover consciousness shortly."

Holcomb held the smile on his lips. "You men carry the captain to his boat," he said. "No, Spider, he won't be conscious for some while unless his head is harder than I think it is." He weighed his gun in his palm. "A stubborn man, if you'll help me… the boat deck."

The boat deck was in turmoil. A group of men in a tight, silent wedge was rushing for one of the boats. Holcomb shouted an order and one of the men fired at him. Though his bullet went wide, Wentworth lunged into swift and deadly action. The man fell, his heart shattered by the Spider's lead and Wentworth was among them striking on all sides with his guns. His eyes were tight with anger. He suspected that these men were the poisoners… Within a few moments, he had smashed the attack. The men retreated, fleeing wildly in all directions. After that, the abandonment of the ship went forward more smoothly. Wentworth hurried from boat to boat, helping the passengers, carrying out Holcomb's orders. Only once was there any more disturbance. Five men in stewards' garb rushed a boat that was just beginning to fill. A woman with a child was hurled to her knees, an old woman battered against a davit.

Wentworth was under the men like a fury. He caught the leader by the waist, lifted and hurled him overboard, faced the others.

"If the rest of you are in a hurry to leave the ship," he said pleasantly, "you can leave by the same route!"

The men shrank back and the example crushed any other

revolt that might have been breeding. Wentworth stooped to help the woman and her child tenderly to their feet, to assist the old lady. She was spluttering indignantly, a quaint bonnet awry on her white hair.

Wentworth laughed, "They were merely impetuous," he said. "I think their leader is cooled off sufficiently now." He tossed a life preserver overboard to where the man bobbed on the surface of the quiet sea.

The old lady's hand came hesitantly to Wentworth's arm. "I've heard some awful things about you, Spider," she said timidly, "but, land sakes, I don't think I believe them. I think you're a nice young man." She took his arm. "You may help me into the boat."

Wentworth did as she requested, stooped to kiss her withered fingers as he left her and felt her hand tighten on his. Her eyes looked trustingly up into his masked face.

"A nice young man," she repeated.

Wentworth sprang away from her with a furious energy as he continued his work, but his heart sang within him. It was good to find that there were some who did not fear the Spider, who could find good in a man who must often kill to protect ravaged humanity. There was a song in his heart, but there was a choking in his throat, too....

When the last of the women had been placed in the boats and the men were filing in orderly fashion to their positions, Wentworth found Nita waiting quietly for him. They slipped away together and, disguise stripped off, found a place in a boat. It was strange that the Spider could vanish from a liner at sea, the people thought. If Holcomb suspected any connection between the man who arrived by plane and the masked, becapped figure who had fought beside him, he kept his mouth shut. And he did not know the man's name....

CHAPTER 6
DOCTOR OF MURDER

FOR WENTWORTH and Nita the days that followed were horrible. It was true that he had averted a great tragedy at sea, but there were many on land that he could not even suspect. On every side men and women died of the fearful poisons and the cases were no longer hidden thanks to Wentworth's vigorous insistence through the newspapers on investigation in every death. Still he could trace no connection between these poisonings and any of the persons he had come to suspect.

His further investigation of Dr. Moreland had yielded nothing and Hess produced carbons of his reports showing that he had told Kirkpatrick that the designated victims had been poisoned. Police could find no trace at all of these reports, nor could Kirkpatrick's lawyers discover them among his papers. Kirkpatrick himself continued in his comatose condition, with recurrent, but helpless periods of consciousness. Wentworth ceased to visit his bedside when Dr. Higgins declared he thought the excitement they engendered was bad for his patient.

Jackson's surveillance of Charles Skeer, whose family had been poisoned, was so far fruitless. The private detective, Oscar Marsh, who had visited the ship's doctor just before the latter's suicide had been innocence itself.... Yes, it was a hopeless

"Why, Good God! The cadaver wore the face of... of Blackie Davis!"

outlook—and the death toll from the wholesale poisonings had passed a thousand—when the first tangible lead developed. Jackson telephoned hurriedly that Skeer had just slipped out of a side entrance of his home and apparently had attempted to disguise himself by wearing battered old clothing. He had taken a taxi and sped to the East Side....

"Nice work, Jackson," Wentworth said swiftly. "I'll join you at once!"

There was buoyancy in his step for the first time in days as he hurried along the hall, calling for hat and cane. Nita heard the jubilance in his voice and met him at the door. Joy for him—but for her—worry and apprehension until his return, for she knew that he went into dire peril; into the face of death itself.... She turned abruptly and ran to her room, was back in a trice pulling a close hat over her rebellious bronze curls.

"Don't say a word," she told Wentworth vehemently, "I'm going with you!"

Wentworth laughed, tucked her hand under his arm. "My shield maiden!" he cried. "I wouldn't leave you behind if I could!" God knew he drew strength from her presence, an inspiration that was as deep as love. She had fought by his side in many a close battle, and her hand was almost as steady as his.

Wentworth's powerful Daimler waited at the curb and Nita sprang into the front seat beside Ram Singh while Wentworth entered the rear. Instantly, the car was in motion and, behind the drawn curtains, Wentworth once more assumed the disguise of the Spider. He pressed a button under the cushion's edge and the left half of the rear seat slid quietly forward, revolving as it advanced. In its back was a close-hung wardrobe, a tray of make-up materials with a neon-light mirror which folded upward. Wentworth hummed lightly as the sinister face of the Spider once more appeared over his own. There was a singing power in his blood. Battle at last, the battle he loved, lay ahead of him; an opportunity to fight for his people against the dogs of the Underworld!

He had been right about Skeer, he was positive now. The man must have arranged with the poisoner to remove his family, or else he was himself a member of the dread organization which was spreading death over the entire city. Why else should Skeer have slipped from his house in disguise and sped into the squalid East Side? Oh, perhaps the Spider was too sanguine. But there must be a break soon in the case. There must—or fear would empty the city of its millions and cripple the commerce of a nation!

AT THE point from which Jackson phoned, Ram Singh slid to a halt and raced for a telephone. He came back and leaped to the wheel again, after telephoning Jenkyns at Wentworth's apartment.

"West again, *sahib!*" Ram Singh tossed over his shoulder. "Jackson says Skeer *sahib* is doubling clumsily as if to avoid pursuit. He does not think that he has been seen."

The chase was long and torturous, but ultimately it ended at a saloon on the lower East Side. Jackson strode to the car from a dark doorway.

"Still in there, Major," he reported swiftly. "Talking with Blackie Davis, who was waiting for him."

Wentworth nodded, his eyes sharpening in the darkness of the tonneau. Davis was called Blackie, ironically enough, because of his blackmailing record as much as for the swarthy darkness of hair and complexion. He was suspected of two or three murders, of the type that gangland had made famous, the butchering of a helpless man. Wentworth laughed softly, "Excellent," he said. "I am glad that it is Blackie Davis. When Skeer goes, get Davis outside, Jackson, lead him along this street. I'll step out of the dark and grab Davis. You run, Jackson. Ram Singh, get the car out of sight and follow."

Nita started to step out beside him, but Wentworth sent her back gently. "Davis is a coward, darling," he said, "but he can shoot. And what happens after he tries may not be pretty...."

Nita resolutely forced a smile to her lips. "All right, Dick," she returned quietly. "I'll keep in sight and if you need me...."

"If I need you, I'll signal," Wentworth nodded. He crossed the pavement and vanished into the shadows against the buildings; the Daimler rolled off into the night.... It was an hour before Jackson, reeling beside a slighter man who walked with an effect of eternal wariness, came out of the saloon. They stopped to argue drunkenly just outside; then they turned up the street Wentworth had indicated. The capture was simple, a leap from the darkness, a wrist-lock and a pistol grinding into the man's ribs.

"Be quiet, Blackie," Wentworth commanded softly. Jackson galloped off up the street, giving a fine effect of drunkenness. Blackie stood still, trembling, then obeyed the pressure of the gun and walked to the rented coupé Ram Singh had brought.

As he stepped in, Wentworth tapped him lightly behind the ear with the gun barrel. While Blackie reeled, half-dazed, Wentworth handcuffed him to the door-post, got under the wheel and rolled it swiftly away. He drove in silence, not even looking toward Blackie, his grim profile set with a sinister smile.

Blackie Davis quickly recovered from the blow. He cast frightened side-glances at the black-caped figure beside him and his terror increased. He recognized his captor. The silence continued and the coupé took the ramp of the bridge into Queens.

Blackie spoke for the first time. His voice came out thin and shaken. "Wh-what do you w-want with me, Spider?"

Wentworth swung his head about slowly and smiled at Blackie, then looked ahead again. That smile was a curious thing on the lipless mouth. It was not reassuring. Blackie's trembling increased.

"Spider!" he whispered. "What do you want?"

Wentworth shook his head and drove swiftly on. He turned off the bridge and began to wind through the deserted streets of the warehouse district. He stopped finally beside a vacant lot, leaned over and unlocked the handcuffs. He could hear the clicking of Blackie Davis' teeth, see the terrified shine of his eyes. The Spider drew a gun.

"Get out, Davis," he said softly. Blackie cried out hoarsely. "No, Spider. No! What do you want to kill me for? I ain't done a thing!"

WENTWORTH PERMITTED his lips to smile again. "Kill you, Blackie?" he asked gently. "Who said I was going to kill you? It seems to me that the right front tire is low. I want you look at it for me, Blackie. You wouldn't mind doing that, would you?"

Blackie hunkered down in the seat and braced his legs. He beat his fists on his thighs. "For God's sake, Spider. For God's sake! What do you want to kill me for?"

"But I don't want to kill you, Blackie. Why would I want to kill you?"

"God, Spider, don't talk like that! I ain't done…."

"Nothing at all. I know, Blackie. You just took money from Charlie Skeer, payment for killing his whole family. But that's nothing at all, at all."

"Spider! I swear…!"

Wentworth laughed, the flat, mocking mirth of the Spider. "Since you have done nothing, my dear Blackie, why you have nothing to fear from the Spider. Just get out and look at that tire…."

Blackie Davis sat very still, his breath whistling through his nostrils, his fists pressing against his thighs.

"Get out, Blackie…!"

"Spider, listen to me. Spider!" Blackie turned and tugged at Wentworth's sleeve, plucked at it with trembling fingers. "Listen, Spider. I swear I didn't know nothing about that. I didn't even know who the guy was. I just got orders to go to Jack's saloon and get an envelope and take it to…" He broke off, shuddering. "God, Spider, that's all I know…."

"Of course, Blackie." The Spider's voice was cunningly soothing. "Of course. And since you know nothing, there is no reason to kill you. *Get out!*"

"I won't! I won't!" Blackie was crying, hysterical. "I won't get out. You can't…!" He broke off, panting. The Spider's gun came toward him slowly, the Spider's face thrust toward him.

"I can put you out without touching you," Wentworth said softly. I can open that door and put you out without touching you. Blackie, do you know how I can put you out?"

Blackie sighed and sagged down limply in the seat. "All right," he whispered hoarsely. "All right. I'll talk. I was going to the Wilson Mortuary Parlor and ask for the Doc, and I was going to hand over this envelope to him. You got to say, 'I'm a sick man and before I get sicker, I want to see the Doc.' See?"

Wentworth's hand shot out, the gun dropped, the forefingers forked and rigid. The fingers jabbed into Blackie's throat and he collapsed into an unconscious heap without a sound. Wentworth sprang to the street and sent a shrill, wailing whistle into the night. He heard a motor murmur into life and moments later the Daimler rolled around a corner and romped toward him. Into its back, Wentworth hauled the limp Blackie. While he worked, he talked with swift economy of words, telling what he had learned from Blackie. Ten minutes later, there seemed to be two Blackie Davis' in the back of the car, but one sagged laxly on the seat, and the other sat briskly erect before a make-up mirror.

The man before the glass—it was Wentworth in disguise—hopped to the pavement beside the car. He took a few slinking steps, twisted about half-furtively and whined. "God's sake, officer, I ain't done nothing. You ask him if I done anything. Just a few drinks…."

Nita clapped her hands. "Perfect!" she applauded. "You're Blackie Davis to the life! Now what do you want us to do?"

Wentworth came swiftly to the car again. "Davis is undoubtedly late for his appointment now," he said. "I don't dare delay any longer. Give Davis a shot of morphine and follow me in the car. Keep him with you. I'm going to Wilson's Funeral Parlor and meet 'the Doc.' When I do...."

HE LEFT the sentence hanging in the air, raced to his own coupé and whipped it at furious speed through the streets. He knew Wilson's Funeral Parlor. It was gangland's favorite, the place from which they buried their enemies with long processions of gleaming cars and wagon loads of flowers. It was curious that the Doc, who must be either the head of the poison ring, or one of its leaders, should choose such a place to receive reports from his underlings.

Wentworth's hand went to the gun under his left arm. If he should prove to be the leader himself.... But the man must be made to talk first. Somewhere, the man must have great stores of deadly poisons, and his destruction alone would not stop the operation of the murderous gang he had assembled. There was no time to examine the envelope which Davis had received from Charles Skeer. Any tampering with it would probably excite suspicion anyway.... Twice, Wentworth had to slow his pace to make sure that the Daimler was keeping pace, but he need not have worried. Ram Singh would have cut off his right hand rather than fail his master in the slightest....

Wilson's Funeral Parlor had a brilliantly lighted marquis, and its window featured a huge floral rendition of "Gates

Ajar." Wentworth stopped his car two blocks from it and hurried on afoot, moving with the furtive wariness of Blackie Davis, glancing again and again back over his shoulder. He ducked into the door, mumbled the formula of admission to a suave, hand-washing Greek who met him, and was ushered through a draped hallway to the laying-out room of the undertaking shop—and halted in his tracks, clamping his teeth to choke down hard a gasp which was almost forced from his throat.

The room was empty save for a coffin on a trestle and he could just glimpse a pale blue shroud. The Greek had dropped back and he stood alone on the threshold of the room. What was expected of him? Blackie had given no more of the formula of admittance than he had used... He threw a glance over his shoulder as Blackie might do, then sidled forward until he could gaze into the coffin. It was a woman who lay there, but it was plain that her face was covered by a mask. Not the domino of a masquerade, but a death mask of clay covered her entire face....

Wentworth fought for self-control as he looked at the mask, for the face there was the face... of Nita van Sloan! It was fantastic, ridiculous, but he could not fail to recognize the sweet, brave lines of her face. Good God, had be been discovered already? Had the Doctor taken this means of informing him that he was in a trap? Wentworth swallowed stiffly, feeling the hard pound of blood in his right temple, where an old knife scar had left its trace. Once more, he glanced about him. In his masquerade as Blackie Davis he could do that. About him, nothing moved. The drapes of the walls did not stir. Rapidly, he mumbled again the words about having to see the Doc.

The effect on the shrouded woman in the casket was immediate. She sat stiffly erect, her right arm lifting and pointing across the room toward a far corner. How must he act? Blackie Davis, if he had never seen this rigmarole before, would be terrified. Was he supposed to have witnessed such a scene before? Wentworth had no way of telling, but he could alibi a showing of fear if the real Blackie had undergone this trail before….

He stumbled, almost fell, in his eagerness to reach the corner toward which the woman pointed. As he moved away, the girl sank back into the coffin, and Wentworth found that he did not have to simulate the whiteness which underlay his lean cheeks or the perspiration that beaded his forehead. It was not that the mummery frightened him, but for a moment, gazing down on that face which was so like Nita's own, he had known a deep shock. Always, Nita faced deadly peril when the Spider battled against the Underworld; always he feared for her life, and that shrouded figure in a coffin had seemed terribly prophetic. The hair was deep brown with bronzy lights like Nita's own, the trim body… And what was the meaning of the masquerade?

WENTWORTH THRUST such thoughts firmly from his mind. He could not speculate on those mysterious things and maintain the peak of his efficiency, as he must if he were indeed to face the leader of the poison ring—and not only fool but overpower him…. Behind the curtains the girl had indicated, he found a doorway which, opened, revealed ascending steps. He went up them, with a swiftness that might well personify

Blackie Davis' fear. The room at the top of the steps was in darkness, but as he stood there, waiting, a green glow developed out of the blackness about him until the stood in a column of ghastly light which flowed from ceiling to floor. There was no other movement, no other light, and once more Wentworth knew a touch of queasy apprehension about the possible discovery of his trick. First of all, the disguise of the woman below stairs and now this long, hidden scrutiny. Was he supposed to give some signal now? Or was there something on the person of Blackie Davis that would reflect this greenish glow and thus identify him? Wentworth wore Blackie's clothes, but....

He realized abruptly that another patch of greenish light was developing in the darkness ahead of him. It seemed to originate not in floor or ceiling, but at a spot about midway between them. At first it had no form at all. Then, abruptly, Wentworth realized that he was looking on the naked cadaver of a man; that the corpse seemed to throw off the greenish glow as if, putrefying, its phosphorus content had concentrated in the skin....

Wentworth felt a sharply rising impatience, but held himself rigidly in check. All this mummery was intended to impress the minions of the Doctor, and this false Blackie Davis must likewise be impressed. He dragged off his hat and scrubbed his forehead with his sleeve. If only he knew whether Blackie Davis was accustomed to this mode of gruesome welcome....

The appearance of the second presence—a living man, was instantaneous as the birth of light in darkness when an electric bulb is turned on. One moment, that corpse floated alone and horrible in the darkness, and the next moment, the other man

95

was there, a man who wore the white robe, the white hat and mask of a surgeon, whose hands were covered with the rubber gloves of the operating-room. In the glow, all these things were a ghastly green…. The shadow of the mask obscured the man's face, but his eyes gleamed from the shadow.

The man stood motionless, once he had entered the aura of green. There was a scalpel in his right hand, Wentworth saw, and he apparently was ready to begin a dissection….

Even while Wentworth's brain raced with conjectures about his own position, with speculation as to what his next move should be, he knew a moment of admiration for the man who had staged this scene with such care. The disguise was complete, the face fully obscured, body, hands and hair covered by the antiseptic robes.

"Well, Davis?" the surgeon said, voice deep, muffled by the mask.

Wentworth ducked his head in a jerky nod. "I got it, Chief… Doc, I mean." He slipped a hand into his inner pocket and drew forth the envelope, but made no effort to advance. He thought he detected movement in the oddly concentrated darkness about him and, without other warning than that, the envelope was snatched from him by a hand that flicked into the green aura and was gone. A few seconds later, the envelope was proffered to the doctor out of the darkness and he took it, laid it on the chest of the cadaver. His eyes remained focused on Wentworth….

THE SPIDER held his face twisted into the awed, half-frightened countenance of Blackie Davis, but his keen brain darted about seeking a way to success. He had no way of telling how many men besides the Doctor were in the room. At least one other, but any number might be lurking in the darkness, for the green light had the peculiar quality of entirely blinding him to all other parts of the hall in which he stood. It would be useless then to whip out his gun and kill the Doctor. He had small doubt of his ability to do that, but, alone, it would accomplish little. He could not even be sure that this man, the Doctor, was the real leader of the poisoners....

Wentworth became aware that the light about the doctor was changing slightly and abruptly he realized that it was concentrating on the face of the cadaver over which the Doctor poised his scalpel. Why, Good God! The cadaver wore the face of... of Blackie Davis! Wentworth's thoughts shot back to the fact that he had been compelled to wait a while to see the Doctor, that the Daimler had not followed him closely for the last several blocks of the distance, and had not shown at all while he was walking the final two blocks to this place. Was it possible that the Doctor had penetrated the trick? That he had had men trailing Blackie Davis at all times? Of course he had. No leader, regardless of his strength, would trust a man like Blackie Davis with money without keeping guard over him. Wentworth was abruptly sure that the man on the table was really Blackie Davis. Then the woman downstairs was...?

But it could not have been Nita! That was impossible. Wentworth told himself that almost with a vehemence of spoken words. "Impossible...!"

The Doctor laughed, and the sound was harsh and cruel. He

put the point of the scalpel above the heart of the cadaver and thrust firmly downward. Blood spurted....

"You see," he purred, "I have killed Black Davis. Can you guess what your own fate will be... Spider!"

CHAPTER 7
THE CORPSE THAT WALKED

WENTWORTH DID not need the challenging words of the Doctor to warn him of his predicament. The fact that blood spurted beneath the scalpel thrust proved that the man upon the table was actually Blackie Davis, still under the influence of the morphine that had been injected into him at Wentworth's orders. In the same instant of realization, he acted. But he went into battle with a torturing doubt in his mind, with the memory of that masked woman's body in the coffin. True, Nita would not have obeyed the man's orders, but if he had drugs which would create catalepsis, why not drugs that would make a person's will subservient? That woman in the coffin *might have been Nita!* The strange—awareness, the tingling recognition that had stirred him there beside the coffin came back to haunt him. He had felt then that the woman was Nita, and he had scoffed at the fact as impossible. But now, now...?

Doubt remained with him as he dived head-foremost out of the spot of glowing green which illuminated him for the gunfire of whatever allies the Doctor had concealed in the darkness. He curled his head under, struck on his shoulders, bounded at once to his feet and checked short, took two long strides to his left.

His first movement had been noisy, but now he was as silent as his namesake, the spider. And no guns spoke, nothing occurred to interrupt his progress. The spots of green light had faded away as instantaneously as he had acted—and there was only the breathing blackness about him.

Wentworth had battled too often in the dark not to know the absolute necessity for orientation. He knew, as he stood there waiting, the exact position and distance of the stairs, of the table with the cadaver of Blackie Davis. He strained his ears and he could hear the slow drip, drip of the man's lifeblood... But the Spider could not remain motionless. Death was all about him. At any moment, the room might blaze with light and blazing guns. Wentworth, waiting, peering into the darkness, permitted a smile to part his lips. He almost laughed. It was considerate of the Doctor to provide the Spider with means of escape. It needed only a few minutes more of darkness....

The muffled voice of the Doctor was laughing off there somewhere, the direction indeterminable. The words he uttered tautened Wentworth's muscles as he went swiftly to work. The Doctor was apparently talking to Nita, and her soft, sweet voice was answering him with a listlessness, an utter humility which stirred savage anger in the Spider's heart. Oh, the man was clever, playing with his enemy before he destroyed him. What chance did the Spider have in this pit of darkness, surrounded by his enemies? He froze, listening. Was he mistaken, or had a snake hissed somewhere nearby? But he could not pause. He could not tell how long this dark period of grace might last....

He sent his voice harshly into the darkness. "You may hold

me prisoner," he cried, "but you'll never take me alive to torture! No man will ever take the Spider alive. Damn you, call off your snakes!"

He fired his gun into the darkness, sent an almost hysterical peal of laughter shrilling from his throat.

"Think you've got me, do you?" he cried. "Not you, nor anyone else. God, snakes! I…!" The gun blasted again and when it's crashing echoes faded there was a long moment of silence, then a gasping breath and the sound of a soft body falling.

The Doctor's voice had died under the assault of those hysterical shoutings. It rang out again, "Lights! Damn you, lights!"
DAZZLING WHITE lights blazed out from the ceiling of the room. It was barren, except for that wheeled table in the middle with the corpse of Blackie Davis upon it. No windows, no doors except the one at the head of the steps—and across the floor four fat-bodied reptiles slid and crawled as if fighting to get away from the light! On the floor lay another Blackie Davis, gun in his right hand. The clothing across his chest was smoldering where a bullet had been fired at point blank range into the heart.…

The Doctor strode jerkily forward, harsh curses ripping his throat. Men scampered about with forked sticks and bags catching the four poisonous snakes and the man in the surgeon's gown and mask stood over the inert body that still grasped the gun. He kicked it violently and the hands jerked and skidded over the floor, slumped back more limply than before. Here was death. There could be no doubt of that. Here was death as surely as when his scalpel had plunged into the breast of Blackie Davis there on the table where the nude body still lay....

Slowly, the Doctor calmed. He threw back his head and laughed. "Who would have thought that the Spider was a coward?" he jeered. He shook his head, gestured jerkily to his men. "Get out of here. If the police come, they must find no one." His men scampered toward the steps as if they feared the sound of his voice and the Doctor still stood over the body on the floor. He nodded, laughing under the mask.

"By God, I'll do it," he whispered. "I'll embalm the Spider's body and keep it as a curio; something to show my grandchildren so they'll realize my greatness, by God...."

Behind him, a soft voice said, "You won't have any grandchildren, Doctor!"

The Doctor whipped about. The nude corpse on the table was sitting erect. In its left hand was a heavy automatic and the muzzle was dead center on the Doctor's heart. The eyes above the surgical mask were strained wide, shining with shock and terror.

He stammered: "But I... I stabbed you! I put the scalpel through your heart!"

The man on the table laughed and the voice was the voice of Richard Wentworth! "Not *my* heart, doctor!" the man said. "You stabbed that man on the floor, who now wears the clothes in which I came here. The bullet hid the scalpel wound very nicely. Foolish of you, Doctor, to try to torture me in the darkness. Foolish of you to give me an opportunity to think...."

Wentworth, for it was he who had changed places with the

NITA VAN SLOAN

cadaver of Blackie Davis on the table, slipped to the floor and walked forward. In his right hand, across his fingers like a sword, he held the Doctor's scalpel.

"No, don't say a word, Doctor. There is really nothing you can say. Take off the gown. That's right. Now the cap and, yes, the mask, Doctor."

The man had doffed the gown readily and the cap. His hands

went to the mask and Wentworth saw with a curse that there was a ring on the man's left hand, and that he was working that hand under the mask toward his mouth. He knew what that gesture portended, knew that the man was about to poison himself, or else take the catalepsis drug. But he must not! First he must talk, must tell where Nita was and by what means he had enslaved her will, how to save Kirkpatrick, where his store of drugs was….

With a shout that was a curse, Wentworth leaped at the man, swinging the automatic, and the lights clapped out in the room, and the Doctor faded away from under his charge as if he were no more than a wraith of fog. Wentworth's feet scuffed the gown he had discarded, but the man himself sprang away without a sound.

WENTWORTH SNATCHED up the gown, raced toward the steps. The door was unfastened, but the Doctor was not there, nor could he hear him moving anywhere else in the room. Damn it, the man must not escape! Throwing the gown over his head, holding a hand before his face, Wentworth raced

down the steps and into the room where the woman had lain in the casket. He reached the coffin in a bound, snatched at the mask upon the figure's face. The girl sat erect, staring into his face. She screamed, the coffin teetered on its trestles and crashed to the floor, and Wentworth stood rigid for a moment, staring. The woman in the coffin was not Nita. It was Dr. Moreland's nurse, Caroline Tarbell!

The woman's scream echoed through the building with a sound of complete emptiness, as if no soul had ever occupied the building, nor ever would. In a half a dozen leaping strides, she banged into the curtained wall, recoiled, then ducked under the hanging drapes and disappeared. Wentworth was already in pursuit. He whipped aside the curtains and stared into a hall no more than ten feet long. There was an empty casket on the floor and no door opened from it, yet Caroline Tarbell had disappeared!

Wentworth whipped about, regarding the emptiness of the room. The quarry had fled. There could be no doubt about it. In some way, the Doctor had contrived to give the alarm. He and all his helpers had fled from the building. And yet it was strange that they would run away when an ambush might have destroyed their arch-enemy, the Spider. Strange, too, that the Doctor should have given a signal to desert the building when, if he were able to signal anything, it should have been to call men to destroy the Spider...!

Realization more swift than thought swept over Wentworth. His lips shut tightly and he bounded across the room toward the door which should lead to the street. He yanked at the knob and it did not yield. His eyes tightened. This was confirmation. Beyond a doubt, this entire structure was to be destroyed, and him with it, unless he escaped within a space of seconds… He stepped back and his gun bucked in his hand, lead smashing into the lock. His shoulder smashed into the door, hammered it wide and he pitched out into the street, fell sprawling. A gun blasted from the shadows, streaming hot lead at his conspicuous, white-clad figure. Wentworth checked his roll with an out-flung arm, fired once and did not wait to see the result of his shot. He flung to his feet and raced on….

The tremendous concussion hurled him flat on his face. He felt heat like the breath from a furnace sear over him. Then he was up and running again. He glanced back and saw that the explosion had enveloped the entire Wilson Funeral Parlor in flames; that tongues of fire were already towering toward the heavens, licking together and flapping as if in mockery of the heavens. Wentworth crouched into a doorway, an awful doubt rocking him. He had heard Nita's voice with the Doctor. He thought he had heard Nita's voice, and in the moment of discovery of Caroline Tarbell, he had thought that it had been hers. Now he did not know. God, he did not know! Nita's fair body might be burning to a crisp in that intolerable furnace….

Torture twisted Wentworth's heart. He shrank further back in the doorway and could not flee. He *could* not. The red light of the fire probed into the shadows of the street, reflected from windows of nearby houses, shone on the white faces of people staring from their windows and doors. There were a few already rushing to the street… Wentworth's teeth set sharply. Who was that woman there in a blue dress like a shroud, standing in the sheltering shadow of a telephone post?

He slipped from the doorway, crossed the street with mighty strides and gripped the woman's arm, whirled her about so that her face was within inches of his. He stepped back, shaking his head violently. This was madness, absolute madness. First, he had been sure the woman in the coffin was Nita, then Caroline Tarbell had leaped from him and fled when he had torn the mask from her face. And now, now facing him, in a dress of the same kind, her black hair disordered about her face was… *Magda Hess!*

Wentworth shook her violently. "Damn you," he said raspingly. "Damn you, what does all this masquerade mean? First Nita, then Caroline Tarbell…."

MAGDA'S FACE was dead white. "Caroline Tarbell?" she stammered. "She telephoned me to meet her here! She said it was life and death, a poisoning case…!"

Wentworth threw back his head and laughed. "Fool!" he shouted. "Do you think you can fool me with your lies!"

Magda leaned close, peering into his face. "Your voice," she whispered. "I know your voice… I've got it! You're Richard Wentworth! What do you mean about Caroline Tarbell? She phoned me to meet her…."

Wentworth forced himself to calmness. The street was choked with excited people now, with the racket of fire-engines and police sirens. He forced himself to realize that Magda Hess might be telling the entire truth. True, he had caught no more than a glimpse of the girl inside, but she had looked like Caroline Tarbell. It took artistry to accomplish a disguise that would fool Wentworth. The woman's actions had been typical of a girl like Caroline Tarbell....

Magda Hess was begging him to tell what had happened, the reasons for his disguise and his queer garb, for the gun in his hand. Wentworth felt abruptly weary. Yes, Magda Hess might be telling the truth. It would have been deft of the Doctor to summon Magda here, either to be killed or seized on the premises so that her death or capture would throw suspicion on old Dr. Hess... Damned clever of the Doctor to plan for Wentworth's death, yet to have misguided evidence planted in case the Spider escaped. The man was far-seeing. But Wentworth had already known that. When the assassination by the policeman had failed, the Doctor had ready the truck which backed into his path, the poisoned candy in Nita's luggage. His efficiency infuriated Wentworth even while it engendered his respect....

He met Magda's gaze and his eyes slowly widened until he stared like a madman. What was he waiting for? Caroline Tarbell had been there as the Doctor's assistant, and that could mean but one thing: Thomas Moreland was the leader of the poison ring, Moreland was... *the Doctor!*

Wentworth whirled and raced away, circling the fire, heading toward the spot where he had parked his coupé. A block beyond it was his own Daimler, but he hesitated over using either of them. Poisoning lent itself readily to hidden needles, and the Doctor had known these were the Spider's cars. In line with his policy of multiple protection, he might well have prepared the cars against the possibility of the Spider's escape.

107

Wentworth shook his head impatiently, raced to the Daimler regardless. Neither Ram Singh nor Jackson was there…nor Nita. He whipped open the door of the rear, standing cautiously aside, and a man's body slid to the ground. Good God! Ram Singh…! Wentworth dropped on his knees beside the Sikh and saw that the right arm was bare to the elbow and that there were two gashes across the inside of the wrist. Even while he knelt, Ram Singh's eyelids quivered open, his teeth glinted white amid his bushy beard.

"Wah, sahib!" he whispered, "thou art served by mice, not men! A woman overpowered us all." The Sikh pushed himself erect, his strength returning. "A woman spoke with the *missie sahib* and she stepped to the pavement and a snake bit me on the arm. Nay, *sahib,* I do not know whence came the snake, only that it struck. I slew it with my knife, gashed my arm. When I looked about, Jackson and the *missie sahib* had vanished and so had this strange woman."

Wentworth's voice leaped harshly from his lips. "This woman, what was she like?"

RAM SINGH shook his head. Could this, too, have been the work of Caroline Tarbell? Wentworth's lips grew firm with abrupt determination. It seemed pretty certain that Caroline and Moreland were the guilty pair, but he could leave no leeway for error. Ram Singh was on his feet, binding calmly the gash in his forearm; ready again for service.

"There is a woman there on the corner," Wentworth said shortly. "Follow her. Report when you can to Jenkyns."

Ram Singh lifted his cupped hands to his forehead in a

deep salaam and strode away. Wentworth whipped back to the Daimler. From a hidden compartment, he extracted some of the money he always carried there for emergency. Within two blocks, he found a taxi and while the man stared at his crazy garb, ordered him to smash all speed laws on the way to Moreland's home. A twenty-dollar bill waved before his eyes galvanized the driver to action and the cab leaped forward.

Ten minutes later, Wentworth dashed up the walk to Moreland's home and paused. The door stood wide open. Wentworth's teeth set. Had the bird already flown? He raced over the house and found the place torn to pieces. Clothing had been strewn over the floor, drugs spilled in disordered heaps. A memory flashed through Wentworth's brain and he darted down the cellar steps.

At the point where the policeman assassin had fumbled on the day he fled from Wentworth, a doorway stood open. Behind it was a complete experimental laboratory and many racks that had contained bottles and vials of drugs, but no longer did so.

Wentworth's lips twisted harshly. This was confirmation of all his suspicions. If Moreland were not the Doctor, why this hidden laboratory? But he had come too late. In some way, Moreland had been forewarned… Wentworth moved heavily up the stairs, walking cautiously now, feeling the perspiration drying upon his body, the tenderness of his feet from the unaccustomed barefoot running. He made his way to the taxi, gave an address on a side street a block from his Fifth Avenue apartment. He felt drained of all strength, emptied. In the back of his brain was the constant, gnawing worry about Nita. Had she been caught in that holocaust?

The taxi driver evidently thought the mandate for speed still held good. He ripped through the city streets and deposited Wentworth very quickly at the designated corner. "Some speed, eh, Boss?" he grinned, his eyes curious on Wentworth's scanty attire. "Say, I got a overcoat here you can have cheap."

Wentworth shook his head, smiling faintly, paid the man the promised extra fare and limped off along the pavements which were still hot from the blazing of the sun. Thanks to his arrangements at the service-elevator, he would have no trouble getting into the building; he would use the secret door into his dressing room… His shoes pinched and burned his feet as he dragged them on, his face felt tired and drawn as he stripped off the make-up.

He peered through the peephole that was hidden in the organ at the end of the music-room, saw no one and manipulated the secret door of his dressing quarters. He stepped through, moved quietly to the door of the drawing-room and stopped dead in his tracks, staring. The woman seated on the davenport sprang to her feet and whirled to face him, her eyes frightened. Wentworth's own gaze tightened. He bowed stiffly.

"To what do I owe the pleasure of this visit, Miss Tarbell?" he asked.

The girl took a faltering step toward him. "Oh, God," she whispered, "You, too? You also believe that Tommy is guilty?" WENTWORTH STRAIGHTENED and regarded her impassively, though it was hard to hold down his impatience, the inward demand to force her to talk, to reveal the truth about Nita. This was some new trick, of course. She probably had poison on her person ready to put in his drink, or inject into his body… She stood very stiffly, twisting her hands.

"If you won't help me, we're ruined," she said dully. "I found out that the police were coming for Tommy and made him hide…."

"In the secret room in the cellar?" Wentworth demanded harshly.

The girl looked at him and he could see that the words meant nothing to her, or else she was the cleverest actress he had ever beheld… He jerked a hand impatiently. "Go on with your song and dance," he grated.

The girl's lips trembled. "You won't believe, but I must talk. I *must.*" She dropped back on the davenport, and her voice ran on and on. She had met Tommy Moreland at a school in the Midwest where both had been students. Then Tommy had come East to do his interne stint and finally to practice among the society people to whom his family and name gave him access, despite the fact that their fortune was shattered. She had found she could not give him up and had come East finally, studied nursing and managed to get into his office. She looked up at Wentworth, her eyes starry.

"Oh, but he doesn't care for me," she whispered. "I don't mean anything at all to him. Just an efficient nurse. A good helper in his office. That Hess woman, Magda…" She shrugged. "But you're not interested in my lovelorn letter, are you, Mr. Wentworth?"

111

In spite of himself, Wentworth felt sympathy for the girl tugging at his heart. Damn it, she was sincere! He scoffed at himself for the thought, but it persisted.

"Go on," he said gruffly.

"Magda Hess is poisonous," Caroline Tarbell's voice was rough in her throat. "She doesn't give a damn about Tommy, but she's using him in some scheme of hers. I don't know what. I've tried to find out… Tonight, I was listening in on the radio and a police order was sent out to pick up Tommy. I ran to him, made him leave and hide. He didn't want to, but I made him. It was pretty plain that somebody was framing him. Oh, Mr. Wentworth, please help us! If you don't, Tommy is ruined. And he didn't poison anybody. You know he didn't poison anybody." She whipped to her feet, stretching out her hands. "In God's name, help us. Please, oh *please…* " Sobs shook her. Her curly brown head dropped into her hands and Wentworth remembered another curly brown head, and a bravely smiling face. Nita, where was she now…?

He was talking before he realized it. "I went to Moreland's house tonight to take him to account for those poisonings," he said, "but I'm half inclined to believe that, if he is guilty, you're ignorant of it…" He stopped, remembering that his chief reason for suspecting the Doctor was the fact that he thought he had seen this girl in the place where he had come face to face with the murdering genius of the Doctor; that Magda Hess had been called to the scene, apparently by Caroline Tarbell. It was a plot, all a plot; a deliberate attempt to put the blame on Moreland. Even Magda Hess had been dragged into the thing….

"I'll do what I can," he said abruptly.

CAROLINE TOOK a stumbling step forward. She dropped on her knees and caught his hand to her lips. "Oh, thank you, thank you!" she sobbed. "Now, I'm sure we'll win…" Wentworth pulled his hand free, "Get up," he said shortly. He tugged at a bell pull, calling his butler. Jenkyns came and stood stiffly in the doorway and the bell of the outer door buzzed.

Wentworth nodded that he was to answer, and abruptly strode after him. Lord, it might be Nita. It might be Ram Singh with word of Nita. He was aware of Caroline Tarbell hurrying after him. Jenkyns peered through the peephole; then with a distressed cry, threw wide the door. Wentworth stopped dead in his tracks, feeling his heart fall leadenly in his breast, feeling despair bludgeon his soul. The two men who stood between the poles of a stretcher shuffled in and Jenkyns bustled off ahead of them down the hall, leading the way. Wentworth took a step forward and the men stopped, glancing at him with pity.

Wentworth's hand lifted to his throat. He ripped his collar loose with a jerk of his fingers. He cleared his throat, but still the words wouldn't come. Caroline Tarbell slipped past him and bent over the still figure on the stretcher. She looked up into Wentworth's face. Her voice came out with an abrupt loudness, "I can't find any pulse."

Not until then did Wentworth speak. He whispered, *"Nita!"*

It was Nita they had brought in on the stretcher, so white, so motionless she seemed like that other prophetic figure in the coffin….

"I say, Wentworth," a man spoke, "this is bloody awful, what?"

113

Wentworth became aware that Jon Vanderveer was standing awkwardly just outside the door, that he had apparently come with Nita. His monocle dangled loosely about his neck, and he went on talking ramblingly. "I was down at police headquarters, don't you know, doing a bit of the old detecting when a cabbie brought her in," he said. "Knew deuced well you'd want her brought to you." He fumbled in his pocket and brought out an envelope. "This bally thing was in her hand," he muttered.

Wentworth took it dully and ripped it open. No doubt what it contained some taunting message from the Doctor. His mind would not work. Nita, Good God above, *Nita...!*

"It's a message from the poisoners," he said clearly. "She is not... dead. The catalepsis drug has been injected and they say there is a cure." He laughed a little. The sound was uncertain. "If I keep out of the fight against them, they will give me the cure, but otherwise..." His voice died.

Caroline Tarbell jerked to her feet from her crouch beside the stretcher. Vanderveer took a step forward.

"Otherwise...?" Caroline whispered.

Wentworth laughed again. The sound was harsh, full of self-mockery. "Otherwise, the catalepsis drug—*will kill Nita within twenty-four hours!"*

CHAPTER 8
NIGHT OF DOOM

THERE WAS a deadly hopelessness about Wentworth's movements as he phoned for a physician and nurses to

His arms flung wide as he went backward under the impact of the bullet.

115

attend Nita, but he insisted on doing it himself. Movement of any kind, the necessity of speech, kept him from thinking. It was awful to think, yet thoughts would peck at his brain. The letter probably told the truth, at least insofar as it said that there was a cure for the catalepsis—an antidote. And there seemed to be varying degrees of potency, for Kirkpatrick lingered on, his condition seeming not to vary at all, except as he grew weaker. Whereas Nita....

Wentworth checked his hard striding back and forth across the terrace of his penthouse, stood rigidly, his head was wrenched back, his arms hard and stiff at his sides. He could not do this thing to Nita. He could not sacrifice her sweet life. It was little enough to do, wasn't it? Simply to remain out of the battle for twenty-four hours....

The formal outline of Jenkyns' figure appeared in the doorway and moved toward him. A message of some sort? He strode to meet the old butler....

"Police coming up, Master Dick," Jenkyns reported hurriedly. "The doorman thinks they're after the young lady who was waiting for you."

Wentworth stood frowning into Jenkyns' face. After Caroline Tarbell? Well, suppose they were. What did he care? But he had promised to help her, to do what he could. He went heavily into the house and found Caroline crouched miserably on the davenport, her hands twisted whitely together. Her eyes pleaded with him, but she said nothing. Vanderveer was strolling idly about the room, his lanky body more ungraceful than usual, head sagging, monocle screwed determinedly in his eye.

"Come with me," Wentworth told Caroline curtly. He strode into the music-room, shutting the door solidly behind him; then he bound a handkerchief rapidly about her eyes, caught her by the shoulders and whirled her about. As if he were playing some childish game of blind-man's bluff, he jeered at himself, and choked down laughter that he knew held its share of hysteria. When Caroline was dizzy, he walked her to the spot where the panel opened into his secret dressing-room. He was utterly mad to do this thing. She would not know how to find or open the room, it was true. But how did he know he could trust her.

He shook thoughts from his brain and strode to the organ pipes, made the ghost sounds of music rise with hands tapping the sound orifices. The panel in the wall opened and he thrust Caroline through.

"Remain in there quietly," he ordered. "The police won't be able to find you."

Vanderveer was standing discreetly at the far end of the room. "Ripping of you to give the little girl a hand," he beamed.

The police were vicious in the thoroughness of their search, but naturally they found no trace of Caroline. Wentworth continued to stride up and down his drawing-room, too deep in his own grief for resentment. He could think of only one thing. He must save Nita from death. He did not *know* that anything of importance was planned during the next twenty-four hours. Of course not. How could he know? He stood rigidly and laughed at himself. Was the Spider afraid to face the facts, to deal with realism and truth? The issue was plain. During the next twenty-four hours, some unprecedented horror was planned. The

Doctor, to make sure of its success, wished to keep the Spider idle. Probably he would keep his promise to save Nita lest the Spider's vengeance be too horrible, his brain too sharpened by the madness of revenge....

SOMEWHERE, THERE was a dull hammering that seemed almost to come from within his own skull. Somewhere... The devil! It was Caroline hammering on the doors of the secret room which she did not know how to operate. He had told her to remain there quietly... A chill brushed across Wentworth's shoulders and tingled down his arms. There was a wild urgency in that hammering, that demand for exit. In God's name, what was happening in there...?

Every nerve of his body urged him to go racing to her release, but he did not. He went out the main door of the apartment to the other secret entrance that gave on the service stairs. There was the bracket of a light beside it. He loosened the bulb in its socket, then thrusting the barrel of an automatic into it formed a short circuit. The door whipped open and he plunged through. Caroline Tarbell whirled from the other door and ran toward him. Her face, in the dim light from masked wall brackets, was white and distorted. She held a paper in her hand and thrust it before her toward him as she ran.

"They're going to kill him!" she cried. "They're going to kill him!"

He took a paper from her and saw a list of names, the Mayor's, four magistrates, the heads of several departments of the city, the boss of the dominant political party. There was Moreland's, and Dr. Hess's, Jon Vanderveer's. After each name was a notation, a date and an hour of the day and Wentworth realized with a narrowing of his eyes that the date was this very day and that the time indicated was… He glanced instinctively at his watch. Midnight was only an hour and a half away, and midnight was the time after each name. An inner tremor raced over him. Was it possible that this was the coup…?

"Where did you find this?" he demanded harshly.

Caroline's hand trembled as she pointed rigidly to the surgeon's gown which Wentworth had worn during his escape from the funeral parlors where he had so nearly been killed. It was lying on the floor where he remembered throwing it.

"There wasn't anything to do except think," Caroline's voice was muffled, "and I couldn't do that. The surgeon's gown was lying on the floor and I picked it up, to hang it somewhere. Inside of it, this paper was pinned…."

Wentworth felt the blood begin to pump in slow hard surges through his veins. He had anticipated a major catastrophe and he had found it, thanks to this girl. If the Doctor had properly planted his subordinates in official positions, the murder of the men on this list would give him political and police control of the city. Nothing he wished to attempt would be impossible, whether it meant murder, or robbery, or simply graft and racketeering.

He used the same precautions in taking Caroline out of the secret room and led her into the drawing-room before he removed the bandage from her eyes. Even after that, he did nothing right away. His stride lengthened as he paced back and forth, trying to balance Nita's life against those of the men on this list, doomed this night unless he could discover a way to save them. Nita's life... He stopped and stared at Caroline, at Vanderveer.

WENTWORTH TURNED his back on the two and walked slowly out on the terrace. The black sky reached down toward him, sucking up the city's glow as a blotter might white ink. It was soft and cooling here in the darkness while the last ghosts of the day's heat were still vibrant in the air. Off to the east, there was a trembling pulse of sheet lightning. Wentworth wiped it all out with his hands clamping tight and tighter over his eyes. A sound that hurt him, that seemed to come from somewhere near his stomach exploded up through his throat. It battered against his teeth but he would not let it out. This was a hell of a time to cry. He had to make a decision, to meet an issue he had faced before, but which never became easier because it was old. Nita's life against the duty he had obeyed so long, that it had become as familiar and accustomed as breathing—a thing you didn't think about until it became difficult. Even then, it was a thing you did not try to stop. You fought for it. Drowning, you would still try to breathe though your mind knew it would bring death.

He twisted about, back to the night and stared at the patterns of yellow light which his penthouse laid against the night. That quartered oblong up there whose illumination was dimmer than the rest was Nita's room. The shadow of a woman moved across it, a nurse doing what was possible for Nita. Dear God, so little was possible. Tomorrow by this time, if he did not shirk his duty, that light would be extinguished and a sheet would be drawn gently up to hide a face as white. Wentworth's mouth was a straight line whose compressed corners turned downward, seeming to stretch. There was a way, perhaps, a way to serve both his heart and his soul. If he could find the Doctor and destroy him after first extracting his secrets....

Wentworth let the sob come out as a curse. He had to let it out lest it strangle him. Could the Spider win? Could he conquer again, as he had so many times in the past?

Even while his thoughts pounded on through the depths, Wentworth knew that his mind was made up. His hands traveled without volition to the guns beneath his arms. He removed each one in its turn and checked it over; cartridge in the chamber; full clip in the butt; safety on. Then he laughed, loudly, harshly. The Spider had decided to fight, and whom would he fight?

One thing he could do. He could warn the intended victims what was threatened against them. It came to him that it would be useless to inform the police. Their action would depend on Ira Spangler, and he had sufficient proofs of his inability, or lack of desire, to cooperate effectively against the Doctor and his poisons. Perhaps he could assemble all of the threatened men together and with their help plan a defense... He strode again through the room where Caroline and Vanderveer were and went directly to a telephone.

Twenty minutes later, he knew that his plan had no chance. Every one of the threatened men had left his home sometime previously and not one had given his family any clue to his destination! That fact in itself would have warned him, Wentworth realized, even if he had not had the list of names. The Doctor not only planned to destroy these men, but he intended that they should die together in one place. It must be so. These men already had left for the place where the massacre would occur!

Wentworth strode rapidly to the angular detective. "Have you any engagement for tonight, Van?" he asked sharply.

Vanderveer peered at him through the monocle. "Not a bally thing to do," he said vacantly. "Why?"

"When were you at your quarters last?"

"Devil of a while ago," Vanderveer returned amiably. "Luncheon time, I fancy."

WENTWORTH HURRIED him to a telephone to learn if any engagement had been made for him, but Vanderveer's man could call none to mind. Perhaps kidnapping was planned then? Or perhaps Vanderveer had an appointment with some woman whom he did not care to name and that was the way in which he would be trapped. Wentworth nodded his thanks, took a brisk turn up and down the room. There must be a way to form contact with the poisoners. There *must* be…!

Elation struck him sharply. There was a way. Since the woman in the coffin at the funeral parlor could not have been Nita, it must have been either Caroline or Magda. He must frighten both of them so that the guilty one would seek out the Doctor right away. It was as simple as that!

He raced for the phone again, got hold of an official of the company who knew Wentworth's association with the Commissioner of Police and would follow his instructions.

"I am going to call the home of Magda Hess," he said quickly, and gave the number. "I want a tracer put on all subsequent calls. I'll phone you later for the information."

Swiftly then, he got Magda on the wire. He whispered his message, his voice flat and sinister. "Tonight," he said, "the Doctor dies. Tonight at midnight."

He found Jenkyns then and sent him to the street to play his part. He had never used Jenkyns in his work before, but tonight he could not choose. The fate of a city rested upon his success, and Nita's life, too. He told Jenkyns that with hard, quick words. Jenkyns' veined old hand trembled as he picked up his hat.

"You may be sure I shall not fail, Master Dick," he said. "God grant that Miss Nita…" His wrinkled face worked. He closed his lips firmly against trembling and went out.

Wentworth returned vigorously to the drawing-room, fighting with all his strength of will to register triumph and excited pleasure. He faced Caroline….

"Tonight," he cried, "the Doctor dies!"

Caroline started toward him. "What do you mean? What doctor? Not Tommy, oh surely…."

Wentworth snatched up a dark hat from the hall closet, snatched a sword cane from the rack and strode from his apartment. Once he was in the elevator, sweeping downward, the smile left his face. There was a desperate fire in his gray-blue eyes. If he should fail tonight. If he should fail… He rolled his shoulders. There must be not even the thought of possible failure!

He was quite sure that neither Caroline nor Vanderveer would linger long after his departure. They would better not, or all his plans would avail nothing for the men who were doomed this night by the Doctor. Swiftly, he recounted his reasoning. The girl in the coffin at the funeral parlor could not have been Nita. Only Magda and Caroline were left and he had arranged to have both followed. Ram Singh would trail Magda and there was a recording device attached to the phone at home which would repeat his message to Wentworth when he sounded a certain note from a tuning pipe he carried in his pocket. Jenkyns would follow Caroline and Wentworth himself would take the trail of Vanderveer, whom the Doctor had slated for death. If all three failed….

MINUTES SLIPPED past and no one left the building. Wentworth was tense with the necessity for haste, but even when Vanderveer finally made his exit alone a half hour later, he was in no hurry. He sauntered to the curb, hailed a cab nonchalantly with a lifted cane and climbed leisurely into its rear. He went straight to his apartment house and there was nothing to do but wait. After a few minutes of that, Wentworth hastened to a nearby drug store and from a booth called the telephone company official. A girl to whom he assigned the task said… "There were two telephone calls from Grant 9-8234…."

"That's my number," Wentworth interrupted. "The phone I wanted watched was a Jervis number."

The girl's voice was sing-song, matter-of-fact. "I'm sorry, sir, but I have no records for that number." How could she know that the fate of an entire city hung on her task? In God's name, why hadn't he made his instructions more explicit? It was immediately clear to him that there had been a misunderstanding of his request, and now... But who had made two calls from his phone?

He asked the girl to give him the numbers called. One of them was to Magda Hess—that would be his own—the other to... his hand closed painfully tight about the telephone receiver.

"You're sure of that?" he demanded sharply. "Sure that call was to the Madison Mortuary?"

The girl was sure and Wentworth whirled from the booth, his heart bounding with hope. Caroline, then, was the guilty one! There could be no reason to think her calling a funeral parlor was a mere coincidence. Either the Doctor used a different mortuary for each meeting with his subordinates or he had moved to the Madison after the holocaust at Wilson's. If the Madison was not the meeting place where the mayor and his colleagues would be killed, then it was a contact from which the Spider could reach the Doctor. His time was short, but if he moved swiftly... The taxi tires gritted on the street as it got away to a fast start under the stimulus of promised extra fare. Wentworth sat tensed on the edge of his seat while the cab traveled two blocks, then he relaxed into the cushions, his mouth twisted in what might have been a smile. It was a first faint hint of success, but God grant that it prove a good omen! He could make no plan of action for his invasion of the mortuary. Hell, he needed no plans. He had his guns! He directed the driver to proceed straight to the door of the funeral parlor, paid the man off deliberately and walked without attempt at concealment into the main entrance. If he were watched....

The man who came to meet him in the chill formality of the

125

"parlor" was grave as a judge, a man in a Prince Albert coat with nose glasses on a black ribbon. His voice was unctuous....

"Can I help you, sir, in any way?"

Wentworth stepped quite close to him and prodded him in the belly with the head of his cane. "If I press the spring under my finger," he warned quietly, "you will die quite horribly of the poison of the black widow spider. Shall we go into the back room together?"

The man's glasses fell from his nose and grayness crept under his normally ruddy skin. Without a word, he moved backward toward the curtains that swung across the rear of the room. A gun hand batted the drapes aside and two armed men came through.

"What the hell is this?" the first demanded. He had an ugly squint in one eye, a lowering forehead. The other was small and neat beneath a smooth glistening cap of oiled hair. He smiled and kept smiling as he moved to the flank. Wentworth felt a fierce joy leap through him. This was a language he could understand and answer. This was the battle he was hungry for. He did not use the hypodermic needle in the head of the cane, but snapped the gold knob upward under the man's jaw. He reeled backward and Wentworth leaped to the side, his cane falling, both guns flying to his hands. The two who had challenged him need only to twist their guns about to shoot and yet there was a smooth speed, a dexterity in Wentworth's handling of his guns, that gave them pause.

"What the hell is this?" the man with the squint repeated uncertainly.

"I came to see the Doctor," Wentworth told them softly. THE SMILING gunman laughed out loud. The other man grew wary, his eyes held small glittering points of light. "So you want to see the Doctor?" he queried. "You sure you don't mean the undertaker?" It wasn't a threat, Wentworth perceived, but formula to which he was supposed to know the answer. If he could reply to that properly, he would be ushered into the Doctor's presence, presumably. Since he did not....

Wentworth shook his head, "The Doctor. Will you take me to him, or—"

The smiling one was hopped to the eyes with some narcotic. He laughed again and whipped his gun into line. The automatic in Wentworth's left hand convulsed and the man's smile became a twisted grimace. The bullet hunched his left shoulder queerly as if he shrugged in exaggerated surprise; then it spun him about so that he faced the wall. He groped for it blindly, hit it with his face and slid down on his knees in a grotesque attitude of amazed supplication.

The second gunman was a little slower and Wentworth waited deliberately until the other man's weapon was almost in line before he shot. The Spider's bullet removed the squint from the man's left eye. His arms flung wide as he went backward under the impact of the bullet. He dragged curtains down with him and they billowed and settled lazily over the body.

These were some of the men who had spread death and desolation over his city. The pay that they received was of the kind they meted out, though the Spider's lead was more merciful. He stopped once beside each body and to the forehead of each he pressed the butt of a slim, platinum cigarette-lighter he drew from his pocket. When he had strode on into the bare back-room, fully revealed by the fall of the curtains, there glistened a crimson spot on the forehead of each man, a thing of blood-like vermilion with sprawling hairy legs and poisonous fangs—*the seal of the Spider!*

Wentworth knew that he did a damning thing. Police were certain to hear the shots which were separated from the street by no more than a glass window. His mere presence on the spot where the seal of the Spider had been imprinted would almost convict him, and conviction as the Spider meant the electric chair on any one of more than a score of kills.

Wentworth knew that and he did not care. A reckless urge to strike and strike again was upon him. If he struck often enough and terribly enough he would in the end find the Doctor through sheer terror. But it must be soon, soon… Wentworth was not entirely without purpose of plan now. Somewhere in this building must be the man who could bring him to the Doctor.

His thought hurled him through the bare door that the curtains had hidden and into the room beyond whose walls were shelves for the display of caskets. There was nothing here to interest him. He sprang for the door beyond and a flick of movement caught his eye. The raised lid of a casket had dropped and through the wall behind it snouted the muzzle of a sub-machine gun. If Wentworth had been forced to wait for the sound of that dropping lid to warn him, the Spider would have died there in that instant, but his eyes had been quick…!

AS HE glimpsed the falling lid, the black muzzle, he seemed

to trip and lunge downward. His left arm flung out straight and the gun blasted.

It was not for nothing that the Spider had spent long hours on the pistol range which he had equipped with many moving targets of his own devising. On that range he had practiced firing from every conceivable position; falling, jumping, running, even somersaulting. He had been doing that for years, and his guns had become almost a part of his body, a mere extension of the nerve ends of his hands. There was no need to aim. When he squeezed a trigger, the bullet sped true. His first shot spattered against the barrel of the machine gun and wedged it hard against the side of the slot through which it pointed. His second bullet sped through the gun-port. Wentworth hit the floor rolling, came to his feet with guns ready.

A glance was enough to reassure the Spider. He raced on for the back-room, and found it empty. There were no stairs leading upward, but his quick eye caught the ring of a trap-door and he reached it in a stride, whipped it upward. A man was coming up the steps that led almost vertically to the dark pit below. He had a gun in the hand which gripped the ladder, the other was reaching upward to lift the trapdoor, and its opening caught him by surprise. Wentworth did not shoot. He went through the trap-door feet first, heels hammering the gunman loose from his grip on the rounds, sending him crashing to the floor below. The trap-door slammed shut.

Wentworth was instantly on his feet, the beam of a pocket flashlight bathing the man he had felled. He nodded jerkily, thrust the light away and thumbed fresh cartridges into the partly emptied clips of his guns. Down here he would be safe for a while from police interruption.

The space in which Wentworth stood was nearly square and had no door in any of the four walls so far as his hands could determine. Yet the man had not been merely hiding in this pit. He was sure of that. He flashed the light on again, inspecting the soft dirt floor. Half of a footprint came out of the wall to his left, a brick wall that seemed entirely solid. Wentworth frowned at the bulkhead that plainly held a secret door. It refused to yield to pressure. There was no way of pulling it... but wait! A smile touched Wentworth's lips. Because criminals generally came from a strata of life to which soap and water was close to anathema, the Spider would enter this hiding place. There was a brick there which, obviously, too many dirty hands had pressed upon. He pushed the brick and it receded two inches. The door did not move, but Wentworth was afforded a grip for pulling. At the first touch, a section of the brick wall which followed the mortar lines swung gently toward him.

From the darkness of the pit, Wentworth gazed into a room which was in every respect the replica of that one in which he first had faced the Doctor. And there, lounging on a chair against the opposite wall, was a man in surgeon's robe and cap. The mask lay on his lap and he was smoking.

"Well, come on in, Bunny," he said irritably. "Have they had any word from the Doc yet?"

WENTWORTH'S HEAD bowed forward a little, his shoulders hunched. It was quite clear that no sounds of the combat had penetrated down here. It was clear also that this man was not the Doctor himself, but some underling used in interviews, possibly with prospective clients for the murder syndicate. Gun hanging at his side, Wentworth stepped quietly into the room and swung the brick door shut behind him. The man in the surgeon's gown leaped to his feet, clapping the mask to his face.

"Who the hell are you?" he demanded, his voice muffled. "You got no right…!" His voice died. He dropped back into the chair and the mask fell unheeded to the floor. His tongue touched his lips. "Listen, Wentworth, I ain't done nothing to you, see. You got no call to come gunning for me."

"That's what your friends upstairs thought," Wentworth said, and laughed. "Ask them what they think now!"

Wentworth stood very close to the man, looking down at him with his piercing eyes. "You are a friend of a man I do not like," he said. His voice was mild, but under it the man winced. "That makes you my enemy. Where would you prefer to be shot?"

The man was frightened, no question of that, but there was a certain steadiness in his eyes as he met the gaze of the Spider. It took no more than that to convince Wentworth that the man would not talk under threats. It might be that pain would change him… The automatic leaped out and the man tumbled groaning from the chair, but still there was no weakness in him. Wentworth bit down curses. This was the one man here, probably, who would have any knowledge of the Doctor or his whereabouts. Certainly he was important, since he wore the Doctor's disguise. Yet he was the one man it would not be possible to crack. Then he must take the dangerous way….

Men who are used to guns and the handling of them know

131

when another man of similar type is at a disadvantage. It was strange that Wentworth, knowing this, allowed himself to get in a position where he could not bring his gun instantly to bear upon the man on the floor. His prisoner shot up from the floor like an uncoiling spring and his fist caught Wentworth flush on the jaw. There was no time to dodge. Wentworth rolled a little with the blow, but it was not enough. He went slamming to the floor, the gun flew from his fist. For a moment, while the man raced toward the automatic, Wentworth struggled to rise to his feet. He flopped over on his face, with his left hand under him, and went limp. The man in the surgeon's gown caught up the automatic and wheeled.

"Where would *you* like to be shot, Wentworth?" he asked raspingly.

CHAPTER 9
MEN MUST DIE

WENTWORTH'S EYES seemed to gaze at the threatening man without expression. They were half covered by the lids, and like all the rest of his body, they seemed without movement, stunned. Actually, Wentworth watched with a keen alertness. His life hung in the balance in this moment— the lives of all those whom the Doctor had scheduled for death. Yet he had deliberately taken this chance. Had placed himself in a position where the man could gain a temporary advantage. If he could not be forced to inform on his chieftain, perhaps he might help Wentworth involuntarily.

Slowly, the Spider stirred and forced himself up from the floor. He kept his right side toward the gunman and concealed the left hand which held an automatic behind his body so that it was invisible. He looked then at the man and his gun and widened his eyes in simulated fright.

The false Doctor laughed. "How about it, Wentworth? Where do you want it? From here, I could shoot the buttons off your vest."

Wentworth shook his head. "It wouldn't do you any good. In a little while, your big shot will be dead or in jail. The cops know about that little murder party the Doc was planning for tonight. They'll be on hand to knock it over."

For seconds, the man stared incredulously. He managed a laugh. "The cops won't do nothing. You're crazy."

Wentworth smiled. "Sure, crazy. Did you know that the Spider paid a visit to police headquarters tonight?"

"The Spider!"

Wentworth nodded, "Do you still think that the police won't do anything?"

The man had been frightened before, but the color seemed to drain even from his lips at this news. "You mean the Spider... killed Spangler?"

Wentworth looked at him unwinkingly, a slight smile beginning to move his lips. So Spangler was an ally of the Doctor's! Wentworth had more than suspected something of the sort. It was a logical deduction from the fact that Kirkpatrick had been kept alive instead of killed outright.

"So you see," Wentworth was almost whispering, "your wisest

move would be to surrender and tell what you know. It might help you when you come to trial."

"Trial, hell!" the man's voice rose shrilly, "They'll never bring me to trial!" He leveled the automatic at Wentworth's head and pulled the trigger, but Wentworth had read his intention even before he struck. His second automatic whipped from behind his body and blasted a split second before the other man's. The arm pivoted stiffly, fingers stretching, and the gun clattered to the floor. For a moment the man reeled with the impact of the lead, then he gripped his smashed arm and broke into a staggering run. Wentworth waited to pick up his other automatic before he followed the fugitive… There was one defect in his plans. If police had wholly occupied the section upstairs….

He reached the brick door and it was wedged tightly shut. Outside, he could hear the murmur of a voice and he pressed his ear close against the crack of the door. Words came through more clearly now, a telephone number. There was also, dimly, the tramp of feet overhead. The police were in the building. Damn, that meant further loss of precious time! He listened to the man's voice, caught the number and heard a mumble in which only a few words were audible.

"Listen, Doc… Wentworth… Madison place… lousy with cops… Sure, I'll try."

WENTWORTH HAD continued pressure on the door and abruptly it began to move. He realized that it had been wedged shut only by the foot of the fugitive. He caught the door and peered around its edge, could see in the dim light that filtered out that the gunman in the surgeon's gown was crouching up

134

the ladder, easing up the trapdoor. A gun crashed in the close confines of the stair pit, again, again, and the man was gone, leaping upward through the trapdoor.

In a trice, Wentworth was after him. He got his head above the edge of the trapdoor just as a machine gun cut loose. On the back of the surgeon's gown, a zig-zag of red showed. He swerved crazily in his course, slammed against a wall and writhed there, screaming, pinned motionless by the hammer of the bullets. The policeman kept on shooting, and Wentworth saw two men in blue uniforms writhing on the floor... When the machine gun stopped, the dead man still stood upright for a long moment, then he fell straight backward as a tree falls. His body made a wet sound when it hit....

Footsteps were pounding across the floor toward the trap-door at a dead run. There was no time to get back into that hidden room, no time even to climb down the stairs. Wentworth did the only possible thing. He let go and fell, hoping that the pounding feet and the shouting of the police would drown the noise of his body hitting.

Excruciating pain stabbed through his skull. He knew that his right arm was twisted under him, but he couldn't help that. Not now... The darkness that swam up to meet him was blacker than the pit....

Wentworth's first thought, on fighting his way dizzily back through the haze of unconsciousness, was that he had made a thoroughly convincing job of his fall into the pit. The sound of a siren came to him with increasing clarity, and there was a recurrent pain in his right arm. He realized that he was in an ambulance. Presently, through slitted eyes, he made out the bulk of a policeman sitting on the chair beside his stretcher, a gun resting on his knees. But the policeman was not looking at Wentworth. It wouldn't be possible to hit him very hard with a left. Wentworth's left hand snaked out, seized and twisted the revolver in one single, smooth movement. The cop screeched as the trigger guard became a trap which was breaking his finger. He let go and Wentworth, pulling to his knees with the surge of the policeman's movement, hit upward and sideways with the revolver. The cop went backward to the floor, knocked cold, and the gun's muzzle centered on the breast of the interne, who had turned a startled head at the outcry.

"Order the driver to get to Gramercy Park in nothing flat," he shouted, "and I don't care if the siren yells itself hoarse!"

The driver jerked about a frightened face, the ambulance took a corner on whining tires, did that again and they were racing southward at furious speed. The siren whined, howled, swelled until it seemed to split the night… Wentworth, with a shoulder wedged against the side to keep from falling, felt every jar in his right arm, which had been crudely splinted and bound to his chest. There was a throbbing ache in the back of his head and his moment of violent action had stirred a writhing snake of nausea in his belly. He fought it with a grimly set jaw. This was no moment for weakness. God alone knew how long he had lain unconscious there at the bottom of the pit. The very seconds were precious. Somewhere nearby, a heavy bell boomed out a single note, but whether it was the quarter or the half hour, or one o'clock, he did not know. His watch was smashed.

136

Through the fury of pain in his skull, he pulled back fragments of that conversation over the telephone. There seemed small doubt that, as Wentworth had planned, the man he had taken prisoner had telephoned the Doctor to warn him of the approaching raid by the police. The Doctor, when he heard it, would know that there was trickery somewhere, would know that Spangler was still alive… Wentworth shook his head and the pain accelerated. He held his head very still and thought. Now he had that phone number. Grant 9, his own exchange, 4578.

HE STOPPED the ambulance at a corner drug store, dropped out and sent the car scooting through the night. It was the work of a moment to extract the information as to the address of the subscriber who had that number. It was a penthouse above a high hotel on Gramercy Square. Wentworth was a block away, safe in the shadows, when a police radio-patrol roadster dashed up to the drug store where he had phoned. He was out of sight when the men left the shop.

There was no chance that Wentworth, with his bedraggled clothing and his arm in a sling, would be able to slip into the towering hotel as one of the guests. His questing eyes found the yellow face of a high clock in the Metropolitan tower on Madison Square. Ten minutes of twelve, ten minutes of life for those great men who ruled the city, and who, Wentworth felt sure, had been lured to this spot to die. There was no doubt about the intention to murder them, merely the possibility that the Doctor alone, not his victims, was here on this roof. Wentworth abruptly began to run. A block away he found a taxi.

"Take me to that hotel on the corner," he said. "Go around the block...."

The driver stared at him, but shrugged and accepted the order. Wentworth paid him from a fat roll which he held in his hand as he walked into the hotel. He was cursing in a monotone that was plainly audible to the bellhops and the room clerk, who stared at him.

"Damned thieves," Wentworth rumbled, "Just because they think a guy has money, they try a hold-up." He peered with narrowed eyes at the clerk. "Do you think I'm drunk," he said, "and can't take care of my money? I got banged up in an accident and they take me to Bellevue. And what do they do? I ask you, what do they do? They fix my arm up on the street and then when I get there they want money before they'll do anything else. Damned hold-up artists."

Wentworth waved the roll of money. "I don't mind spending money, but I'm not going to be held up by a bunch of two-cent grafters in a city hospital. I want the best suite you got. Hell, make it a penthouse! Luggage'll get here when they unscramble that taxi that was wrecked."

As Wentworth had anticipated, that free display of ample money had done the trick. He might be a little noisy, but there were not many hotels in New York that would be closed to that vulgar display of wealth. Wentworth got a suite with a terrace on the eighteenth floor. It was five minutes of twelve when he walked into the room. He chased the grinning bellhop out and promptly left the room. He had to climb two stories by stairs while pain throbbed and burned through his body. And when he reached the poisoner's quarters, what then? True, he still had his two guns, but he would be able to use only one of them, and the poisoner's men would undoubtedly be there in force. It must be enough....

It was three minutes of twelve when he stood outside the door of the suite. He put the muzzle of his automatic against the lock, squeezed the trigger once and ran against the door. It shuddered away from his shoulder and as he charged through, Wentworth whistled shrilly with tongue against his teeth in imitation of a police whistle. A butler in knee pants and hose turned and fled, but a second one snatched a gun from an armpit holster.

WENTWORTH LAUGHED at him and waited while the weapon came clear, then, when he might have killed the man, he shifted his aim a little and put a bullet through his wrist. He might need—he recalled Moreland's ironic phrase after the policeman had died—to try the poison on the dog before he convinced the Doctor's intended victims of the peril they faced. The thought was a flash through his brain, for he was rushing forward while he shot. As the bullet whirled the butler-gunman about, Wentworth shouldered him in the small of the back and hurled him with staggering haste through a long drawing-room at whose farther end, an arch gave on an elaborate banquet-hall. Men in evening dress were everywhere on their feet, staring toward Wentworth, some frightened, some merely indignant. They were all here, the men who were scheduled to die tonight, even Vanderveer and—Wentworth recognized him with a start of surprise—Moreland, sitting behind Dr. Jackson Hess!

Wentworth set his shoulders against a wall, the butler with

the bullet-broken arm whimpering in pain at his feet, and surveyed the diners with a slow, sardonic smile.

"You were brought here to be murdered, you fools!" he said.

Mayor Rockbridge spluttered indignantly, growing red-faced. "These men are my guests!" he shouted. "Do you dare to insinuate...."

Wentworth smiled at him. He stirred the wounded butler with his toe. "Take Mayor Rockbridge's salad and eat it," he ordered. It was conjecture, of course, that the salad was the dish which contained poison, but the Doctor had scheduled the deaths for midnight, and he would perform at that time if only to impress his subordinates. The salad course had been served approximately two minutes before midnight.

The man cringed against Wentworth's legs as though the salad on the table before him were something that would leap to attack him. Little whimpering cries came from his throat. Wentworth laughed.

"Why, gentlemen, do you think that he shrinks from a simple thing like eating the salad?" he cried. "Do you think that his butler's soul shrinks from such an infringement of etiquette?" He stirred the man with his foot again.

Wentworth's eyes were alert not only on the man before him, but on the two doorways that opened into the room within his line of vision. His gun muzzle was restless. It was not to be doubted that the Doctor had allies here. Wentworth must make allies of these victims. It was ironic that he must force them to save themselves, but if he left the room now—if he were shot now—they undoubtedly would sit down and eat the salad—and die!

"You surely understand now?" Wentworth said persuasively. "This man who shrinks from eating the salad carried a gun and tried to shoot me in the hallway… Can't you guess why?"

CHAPTER 10
BLOOD SACRIFICE

UNEASINESS RAN through the assembled guests. They recognized Wentworth. Many of them were his social acquaintances and all knew his reputation as a criminologist. Mayor Rockbridge stepped forward uncertainly.

"That footman," he said, looking at the man at Wentworth's feet. "I swear I never saw him before tonight."

Wentworth nodded. "No one is accusing you, Mayor. In fact, you were to be one of the victims. Would you mind bringing your salad plate here? I have an idea that your guests are not convinced. Gentlemen, can't you see? You are the rulers of this city. If you were removed—if your subordinates took control—the poisoners would rule the city! Can any of you completely trust his subordinate not to be subject to bribery? Can any of you swear that your subordinate is not already in the pay of the poisoners?"

Mayor Rockbridge brought his salad plate and bent awkwardly, offering it to the footman he had disowned. The fellow's eyes flew about the faces of the table guests and Wentworth could not tell that they lingered on any one of them, though he watched closely. Somehow, the man seemed reassured. He reached out a hand that was not quite steady to the Mayor's plate and fumbled with the fork, carried a portion to his mouth. He chewed it systematically, but with a gingerly touch as if there were glass in it that he feared to break. He looked up at the Mayor and grinned.

"Geez, this is swell," he said, "Tanks, Mayor," He took another forkful, chewed noisily.

Doubt and anger crept into Mayor Rockbridge's face, and Wentworth knew a moment of skepticism. Had he guessed wrong? No, no, it wasn't possible. The man's fear of the salad had been genuine all right. But now….

The footman's jaw clamped shut on the food and a rigidity crept into his whole body. He started to his feet with a choked cry. His eyes glared wildly. He took a faltering step forward, past the Mayor.

"You double-crossed me, damn you!" he gasped. "You double—!"

The words stuck in his throat and he pitched forward on his face, hit the floor heavily. From beside Wentworth, a mocking, light voice said pleasantly.

"Drop that gun, Wentworth. Gentlemen, please be seated!"

Wentworth wheeled to his left, but a gun hit his wrist and the automatic fell from his numbed fingers. He was looking into the mocking eyes of a man in a surgeon's gown and mask, and he realized the trickery that had been employed here. Oh, it was clever, damnably clever. While all eyes were centered on the poisoned footman, his men had sprung from doorways and leveled guns at the entire assembly. Wentworth blamed himself bitterly, but in truth his single gun could have done little against all these men. There were fully a dozen of them, and their weapons included sawed-off shotguns and tommys. The guests slumped into their chairs woodenly, all save one. Dr. Hess faced the sardonic Doctor.

"May my soul damn yours in eternity," he said harshly. He lifted a forkful of the salad as if in a toast and swallowed it quickly. "As God is my witness, gentlemen," he said, "I am innocent!" He stood motionless and rigid through a long moment, waiting for the poison to strike. It did… and terribly. His head wrenched back on his shoulders in the violence of his agony and his hands clutched and tore at his throat so that blood streamed from a half-dozen wounds. There was a hoarse sound in his throat, but it was not breathing. He couldn't breathe. The poison was strangling him to death.

THE AGONY went on and on. Men gabbled incoherent things and jumped to their feet as if to help, but there was nothing anyone could do. Dr. Hess' aged face was tinged with blue, his eyes bulging. He fell to the floor, crashing his chair with him, and writhed there, still making that hoarse, awful sound. Then it was over, mercifully over, though he still lay in that terribly contorted attitude. It was not until then that Wentworth realized he had heard a woman screaming. He could hear her voice shrieking curses and suddenly, violently, she burst through a door that was closed and hurled herself down on her knees beside Dr. Hess' tortured body. She flung her arms about his white old head.

The butler pitched forward on his face, hit the floor heavily.

"Damn you!" she screamed. "Damn you, you promised to give him the cataleptic drug, and you've killed him. *You've killed him!*" It was Magda Hess!

Wentworth's half closed eyes shot toward the door from which she had burst. Was he mistaken, or had a man cried out in a half frightened tone that was abruptly silenced as a man's voice might be if a knife plunged through his windpipe? Hope thrilled through every inch of his body. This was the pay-off. He stepped forward and felt the gun of the Doctor gouge into his back, but he ignored it.

"It is just," he said deeply, "a payment for your sins, Magda. Those who conspire against their parents… *Honda dwarza….* " He spoke words in Punjabi as if he quoted a proverb of the people. "You behind the door, come forth suddenly. Seize the woman and lay thy knife against her throat!" It was a wild gamble, but Ram Singh had been set to follow Magda and behind that door a man had gasped as if such a knife as the Sikh habitually wore had pierced his throat. Wentworth had small time to speculate, for the answer came almost with the last breath of his instructions.

The door thrust open quietly, but swiftly, and from it bounded a lithe, broad-shouldered figure, a turbaned head above a bushy, bearded face. He took two noiseless, leaping strides and an arm was about Magda from behind, pinioning her arms to her side. That grab was part of the motion that pulled her backward so that Rim Singh stood against the wall with her body before him. The long knife was a blaze of steel as it swooped upward and rested lightly against her throat. The hand that held the knife was steady and sure. The edge of the knife moved a little against Magda's throat, so that a trickle of blood flowed down the whiteness of the skin, and Wentworth's lips smiled slightly. There was a pledge and an oath that went with Ram Singh's knife. It should never be drawn unless to draw blood, and he had fulfilled the pledge....

He himself was in action, even before Ram Singh completed his maneuver. The Doctor had whirled at Magda's gasped cry, his gun wavered from Wentworth's side and an instant later, his gun hand went numb under the shrewd *jiu-jitsu* touch of Wentworth's fingers; his side winced from the thrust of the muzzle against his side.

"Don't move, any one of you!" Wentworth's voice rang like a bugle, "or the woman and *the real Doctor* will die!" He felt the start of the man in the surgeon's gown whom he held prisoner. Magda's eyes blazed fiercely into his. She seemed to be talking to him, her voice sullen.

"Listen, Doctor," she said, "you'll damned well follow orders or I'll tell what I know. I've got it all written down and posted where it will be published if I die. You didn't really think I trusted you, did you? Not after I saw you chasing after that poor little fool of a nurse...."

No one answered her. It was clear she did not speak to the man under Wentworth's gun, but he had expected that. Before this, a man in a surgeon's gown had proved to be merely masquerading as the leader.

"You hear, Doctor," he queried clearly. "You wouldn't want

your secrets known, would you, Doctor? You hoods drop your guns! *You heard me!* Drop your guns!"

MAGDA'S EYES flashed over the men and the guns thudded to the floor. Wentworth's eyes glinted. "See that closet over there, with the door open? All of you get in there—*quickly!*"

Wentworth whipped his captured gun into sight and sent a bullet whining by a man's ear. "You first! Into that closet!"

The man flinched and almost ran into the closet. After that, it was easy. The men trooped in, one behind the other, like sheep, and closed the door. Mayor Rockbridge laughed a little shakily as he turned the key in the lock.

"By God, Wentworth," he puffed, "that was a close thing. I think we'd better get out of here."

"Would you mind waiting, Moreland?" Wentworth's voice was suddenly edged. "Vanderveer, I might need your help."

"Really, old chap," Vanderveer's affected voice quivered a little, too. "This sort of thing is quite out of my depth, what, what?"

Magda, the knife against her throat, Ram Singh's strong arm about her, kept her eyes sullenly on the floor as the men filed past her, hurrying, pushing each other in a sudden eagerness to be gone. Wentworth stared fixedly at Moreland and Vanderveer.

"Moreland," he said abruptly, "you're a damned fool. You've let these crooks put you in a position where you couldn't clear yourself of murder by anything less than suicide. You actually carried the poison into three homes...."

"You lie!" Moreland shouted.

Wentworth shook his head. "I didn't say you knew anything

about it… Vanderveer, I'll give you your choice of eating some of the salad or taking a bullet in the heart."

Vanderveer let the monocle fall from his eye, his mouth sagged open. Wentworth eyed him wearily. "Let's drop the performance, Vanderveer," he said. "You've been very clever with it and you had me completely fooled, I'll admit. Even tonight when you brought Nita and grinned behind your hand at my suffering, I didn't suspect you. But I saw fright in your eyes when Magda mentioned the confession she had written. You've been in an excellent position to operate without suspicion, giving your orders to Spangler and knowing in advance every move the police made. Your entree to society helped you locate victims— both those who would pay you to murder others, and those who were worth murdering from a monetary viewpoint.

"And I know, too, now that it was you who killed the policeman in the basement of Moreland's house, both to prevent Moreland's discovery of a cure for the catalepsis from being used, and to punish the man for using the catalepsis drug too publicly and without sufficient reason. I had the body examined and, in addition to the hypodermic mark that Moreland made, there were three minute punctures on his right arm. I suggest to you, Vanderveer, that you had poison needles in a ring you wore and used to kill that policeman.

"I SUGGEST to you that you and Magda were lovers and that you used her to gain information from her father, to falsify the reports when Dr. Hess made his examinations for Kirkpatrick. You were very careful never to be seen with her, but my investigators found the apartment you and Magda rented…."

Wentworth shrugged. He felt a great weariness, despite his joy at having found the end of this long struggle with the prisoners. Nita lay helpless at home, and Moreland's "cure" was purely conjectural. It might very well fail. Within a few hours now, the twenty-four that the Doctor had allotted her to live would elapse… "It doesn't matter that I can't prove your guilt in court, Vanderveer. I know you are guilty. I have no more time for you. Will you take your own poison, or be shot?"

Vanderveer's eyes were no longer vacuous, but held a glittering animosity. He looked toward Magda and her smile was mocking.

"Well, Van, dear," she said sweetly, "will you confess or shall I? You had me fooled, too, damn you! I thought you really loved me."

Vanderveer smiled. He made a peculiar gesture with his right hand and glanced toward the door through which Ram Singh had made his entry. Nothing happened. Wentworth held his gun on the door.

"Vanderveer signaled you behind the door there," he called. "Why not come out?"

The door batted outward, swung shut, and opened again. The foot of a white wheel table thrust into view, and behind it Wentworth saw the white face of Caroline Tarbell and, beside her, Jenkyns' unsmiling old face. They wheeled the table out into the room while Wentworth's heart thudded high and painfully in his breast. He knew, even before he saw the face of the person on the table… *Nita!*

Vanderveer was smiling. "I make you a bargain," he said softly.

"My life and Magda's for the life of the woman you love. I admit nothing, but I can cure her from this catalepsis in which she lies, which will kill her in a few hours more unless I administer the antidote."

Wentworth's lips smiled slowly and Vanderveer's face turned white. He stammered a little, "I'm not asking you to quit the fight Wentworth. Not that. Just give us twelve hours' start, Magda and me. We'll go to the other ends of the earth. You'll never hear of us again. *For God's sake, Wentworth!*"

From beside the table, Caroline cried out, "Oh, Mr. Wentworth, don't sacrifice the woman you love! It isn't worth it. Nothing is worth that!"

Moreland had been like a wooden man throughout the scene, but he whirled fiercely now on Caroline. "What do you know of love?" he demanded harshly. There was a shrillness in his voice. "What do you know of love?"

Caroline stared at him, her face drawn and very white, and then slowly smiled. She walked forward quietly and put her arms about his neck. She kissed him and Moreland shuddered and clasped her tight. "All these years," he stammered. "All these years…!"

"Do you think this is a time for love-making?" Wentworth realized he was shouting at them, but he couldn't seem to help it. He didn't seem to care. "Moreland, can you restore her to life?"

Moreland's face sobered. "I wish to God I could, Wentworth," he said. "I was conceited about that cure, but it doesn't work. It kills."

VANDERVEER LAUGHED. "I have the cure, and no

one else, Wentworth. You deal with me, or you don't deal with anyone. Come on, twelve hours start. After that, you can kill me if you can catch me. Twelve hours start for me and Magda."

Magda was staring at Vanderveer very fixedly, a queer smile on her lips. She said nothing at all. The knife was still there at her throat. Wentworth's lips twitched. His hand, gripping the gun butt, was moist and he knew there was perspiration on his forehead, across his upper lip. He dragged a hand heavily across his face and knew that the hand trembled. He would not look at Nita. He could not.

God, was this last sacrifice demanded of him? That he let Nita die? His eyes burned into Vanderveer's face and he could see the shrinking of the man. It roused a fierce joy within him. This man had killed scores, hundreds of persons with his damnable poisons. He had persuaded Magda to ruin her father, to contrive his death, and it was all trickery. All of a piece with his other treachery. Slowly, Wentworth's hand came up. If Vanderveer got a twelve hours' start, he would never be caught again. He would wait a while and he would practice again his fearful art of poisoning. As for Magda, she was doomed. If she thought that Vanderveer meant her to live… The gun was pointed at Vanderveer's breast, his fingers tightening on the trigger….

It would kill Nita as surely as if this gun were aimed at her heart instead of Vanderveer's body. He was shooting… Nita! A strong shudder trembled over Wentworth's body. The gun swung down. He stood, panting, shaking. Vanderveer laughed and Wentworth shook his head.

"It's going to be hard to do," he said quietly, "but I'm going to kill you. I don't have to do it myself. A word to Ram Singh...."

Magda said gently, "Why torture yourself? I only wanted to see whether you would go through with it. And I know now; you really will. Don't bother with him. I'll revive Nita and afterward you can do as you wish about me. I make no bargain...."

"You shall not!" Vanderveer screamed. "Currying favor for yourself. You know that if you save the girl, he won't kill you! Damn it, Magda, I won't...."

Ram Singh let the knife fall at a gesture from Wentworth and Magda turned and faced him. "I'll need your knife," she said. Once more Ram Singh obeyed and yielded the knife. Magda's movement then was too fast for the eye to follow, but Vanderveer must have guessed her purpose. He turned and fled across the room screaming wildly... Magda took three quick steps forward, whipped the knife back across her shoulder and threw it. The knife was made for throwing, the blade heavier than the hilt, the point heaviest of all. It flew true and terribly. Vanderveer's white face twisted about at the last moment. He saw the knife. He flung up his hands, screaming, spinning, and the blade flashed through between his hands and vanished into his mouth. The hilt clicked against his teeth and stood out from his mouth like a fat, black cigar. Blood spurted out around it, and a gurgling scream. Then Vanderveer fell forward, dead....

Slowly, Wentworth thrust his gun into its holster. He said dully, "You were not lying, Magda? You know the formula?"

MAGDA TURNED a dead face toward him. It was as if that knife blow which had killed Vanderveer had killed her too.

"I have the formula," she said dully. From her bosom, she drew a large vial. "This contains enough to cure a half dozen people of the effects of the drug. One cubic centimeter will be ample. Administer hypodermically, directly into the heart muscles." She gave the vial to Wentworth, turned away and walked toward Vanderveer's body. Moreland stepped forward, fumbling in his pockets.

"I always carry a hypodermic with me," he said eagerly. "Adrenalin, you know. Always had the idea I might get a chance to save some heart-attack victim with it some day. One cubic centimeter.... He went swiftly to work.

Wentworth stood watching. An eagerness he could not repress kept his heart bounding. It could not fail. It must not... In the back of his brain, he wondered. Could he have shot Vanderveer, knowing that it doomed Nita? Magda believed it. Vanderveer had felt it, but could he? He locked his hands together behind him rigidly, watching Moreland make the injection... The cry behind him was muffled, almost inaudible, as if a cry that someone fought to repress had forced itself out through pain.

But Magda was not in pain. There was a joyous smile on her lips now. She was slumped on the floor beside Vanderveer, her body half-propped on his. She was dead by some one of her own poisons. Wentworth smiled on her, dead, as he could never have done living. She had taken the brave way out, the only way for her.

A hand touched his arm and he whirled about eagerly, reached Nita's side in a long bound. Her eyelids quivered and lifted. Nita's eyes were fresh and dewy as if she had just awakened from a long sleep, but she was weak. There was feebleness in the movement of her hand as she lifted it to clasp his own.

"She'll be all right within an hour," Moreland said, his tone professional. "The shock is a little weakening, of course."

Wentworth sagged to his knees, head buried on Nita's breast. God, and he had almost killed her. Vanderveer… Nita's hand rested softly on his head.

"You have… won, Dick, lover?" she asked.

"He has won a great victory," Caroline's voice answered her.

Nita laughed, and Wentworth knew a great and solemn joy. It did not matter now that death had been so close. The Spider had won a great victory…!

POPULAR HERO PULPS   AVAILABLE NOW:

THE SECRET 6
- ❑ 1: The Red Shadow — $13.95
- ❑ #2: House of Walking Corpses — $13.95
- ❑ #3: The Monster Murders — $13.95
- ❑ **NEW:** #4: The Golden Alligator — $13.95

CAPTAIN ZERO
- ❑ #1: City of Deadly Sleep — $13.95
- ❑ #2: The Mark of Zero! — $13.95
- ❑ #3: The Golden Murder Syndicate — $13.95

OPERATOR 5
- ❑ #1: The Masked Invasion — $13.95
- ❑ #2: The Invisible Empire — $13.95
- ❑ #3: The Yellow Scourge — $13.95
- ❑ #4: The Melting Death — $13.95
- ❑ #5: Cavern of the Damned — $13.95
- ❑ #6: Master of Broken Men — $13.95
- ❑ #7: Invasion of the Dark Legions — $13.95
- ❑ #8: The Green Death Mists — $13.95
- ❑ #9: Legions of Starvation — $13.95
- ❑ #10: The Red Invader — $13.95
- ❑ #11: The League of War-Monsters — $13.95
- ❑ #12: The Army of the Dead — $13.95
- ❑ #13: March of the Flame Marauders — $13.95
- ❑ #14: Blood Reign of the Dictator — $13.95
- ❑ #15: Invasion of the Yellow Warlords — $13.95
- ❑ #16: Legions of the Death Master — $13.95
- ❑ #17: Hosts of the Flaming Death — $13.95
- ❑ #18: Invasion of the Crimson Death Cult — $13.95

DUSTY AYRES AND HIS BATTLE BIRDS
- ❑ #1: Black Lightning! — $13.95
- ❑ #2: Crimson Doom — $13.95
- ❑ #3: The Purple Tornado — $13.95
- ❑ #4: The Screaming Eye — $13.95
- ❑ #5: The Green Thunderbolt — $13.95
- ❑ #6: The Red Destroyer — $13.95
- ❑ #7: The White Death — $13.95
- ❑ #8: The Black Avenger — $13.95
- ❑ #9: The Silver Typhoon — $13.95
- ❑ #10: The Troposphere F-S — $13.95
- ❑ #11: The Blue Cyclone — $13.95
- ❑ #12: The Tesla Raiders — $13.95

MAVERICKS
- ❑ #1: Five Against the Law — $12.95
- ❑ #2: Mesquite Manhunters — $12.95
- ❑ #3: Bait for the Lobo Pack — $12.95
- ❑ #4: Doc Grimson's Outlaw Posse — $12.95
- ❑ #5: Charlie Parr's Gunsmoke Cure — $12.95